THE USBORNE SOCCER SCHOOL

Gill Harvey and Richard Dungworth

Designed by Stephen Wright and Neil Francis

Illustrations by Bob Bond

Photographs by Chris Cole

Edited by Cheryl Evans

DTP by John Russell

Consultant: John Shiels,
Bobby Charlton International Soccer Schools Ltd.

With thanks to Phil Darren

CONTENTS

PART ONE
BALL CONTROL

CONTENTS

GETTING STARTED

Good ball control is the first thing that any soccer player needs to work on. It means being able to receive the ball quickly and effectively and then keep control of it, too. This part of the book shows you how to develop these skills. It covers many techniques, and there are plenty of exercises and challenges to try.

A loose shirt with short or long sleeves is good for training in.

WHAT DO I NEED?

Don't wear shorts or sweatsuit bottoms that are tight. They will slow you down.

All you need to practice with are a soccer ball and some markers. Special sports markers are shown here, but you can use just about anything. Wear comfortable clothing such as a sweatsuit or shorts and T-shirt. On most surfaces tennis shoes are fine, but soccer shoes are best for playing on muddy ground.

Shinguards protect you against hard tackles.

Sports marker.

WARMING UP

To have good ball control, you need to be able to move your whole body well. Being able to twist, turn and keep your balance are key skills for many control techniques.

Do this exercise in pairs. More than one pair can play at once. It is a good warm-up exercise which will improve your balance and movement.

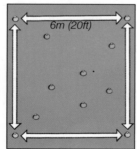

Mark out a 6m (20ft) square. Scatter six or seven markers inside it. Decide who will be attacker and who will be defender.

The attacker dribbles forward, weaving around the markers. The defender tries to stop him reaching the other side.

You cannot touch each other or leave the square. If the defender forces the attacker off the square, he has won.

GETTING THE FEEL OF THE BALL

If you are used to playing around with a soccer ball you will probably already have some idea of how the ball responds when you touch it in different ways. This is what it means to have a feel for the ball. This page looks more closely at how this works and how you can use the different parts of your foot to do different things.

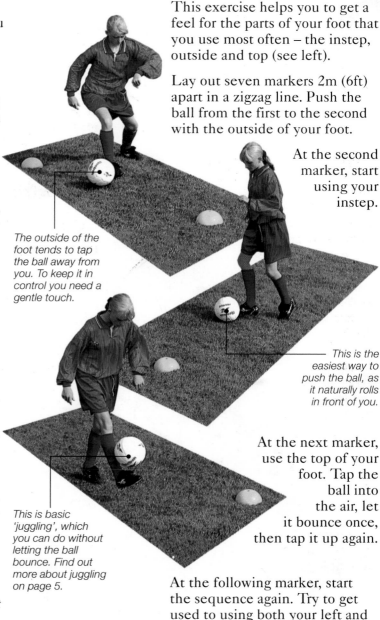

This exercise helps you to get a feel for the parts of your foot that you use most often – the instep, outside and top (see left).

Lay out seven markers 2m (6ft) apart in a zigzag line. Push the ball from the first to the second with the outside of your foot.

At the second marker, start using your instep.

The outside of the foot tends to tap the ball away from you. To keep it in control you need a gentle touch.

This is the easiest way to push the ball, as it naturally rolls in front of you.

At the next marker, use the top of your foot. Tap the ball into the air, let it bounce once, then tap it up again.

At the following marker, start the sequence again. Try to get used to using both your left and your right foot.

Your instep is the part of your foot used most often. Use it for controlling, dribbling and passing.

The outside of your foot is good for turning, dribbling and passing the ball to the side.

The top of your foot, or 'laces', is the most powerful part. It is best for kicking and shooting.

Your heel is not often used, but it is good for flicking the ball backward or a quick reverse pass.

This is basic 'juggling', which you can do without letting the ball bounce. Find out more about juggling on page 5.

It is very difficult to control the ball with the tips of your toes. You should hardly ever use them.

It is risky to use the sole of your foot to control the ball, but you use it for some stunt moves.

CHALLENGE

When you see this trophy, you will find an idea for a challenge. Soccer is very competitive, so you need to keep pushing yourself to improve your personal best for every exercise. Get into the habit of giving yourself new goals each time you do some practice so that you can tell how fast your skills are growing.

MOVING ON

Once you have a basic feel for the ball, you are on the way to developing good control. The next stage is to do plenty of practice to develop your skills. Things like juggling the ball are good for this, but you also need to work on special control methods. Here you can find out about the basic techniques that will help you.

JUGGLING

Although you rarely use juggling in an actual game, it helps you to develop the quick reactions, tight ball control and concentration that you need in order to play well.

To get the ball into the air, roll your foot back over the top of the ball, then hook it under and flick the ball up.

Keep the ball in the air by bouncing it off your foot. Hold your foot out flat. If you point your toes up, you will probably lose control.

As you develop your control, pass from one foot to the other, or bounce it up farther into the air so that you juggle it on your knee.

Keep your eye on the ball all the time.

You could try juggling the ball on your shoulder and with your head.

JUGGLING GAME

Work on your juggling with a group of friends. Choose someone to be a caller. All of you dribble until the caller shouts 'Up!'

Everyone flicks the ball up and juggles. The last one to keep the ball in the air wins. When he drops it, you all start dribbling again.

RECEIVING THE BALL

Controlling the ball as you receive it is one of the most important skills you can learn. Everything else you do depends on this, so it's well worth spending plenty of time on it. These are the main points to remember.

1. To get your timing right, you need to judge the flight of the ball carefully.

2. Don't just hope the ball will come straight to you. Move into line with it.

3. Decide early which part of your body you will use to control the ball.

4. Once you have the ball, don't hesitate. Decide on your next move quickly.

FIRST TOUCH

This player is demonstrating good first touch. The ball is moving and in a good position to be played away.

The moment you make contact with the ball is called the 'first touch.' A good first touch keeps the ball moving and places it a short distance from your feet. To develop this skill, you need to 'trap' the ball.

WHAT IS TRAPPING?

Trapping means taking the speed out of the ball, just as a cushion would if it was attached to your body. It slows the ball down without making it bounce away. Here you can see how trapping works in practice.

As the ball travels toward you, position your foot in line with it to receive it.

On making contact, relax your foot and let it travel back with the ball.

The speed of the ball is absorbed. It slows down and you can play it away.

FOOT CONTROL

Your feet are the parts of your body that you use most often to receive the ball. Remember that a good first touch keeps the ball moving, so use your instep, the outside of your foot, or the top of your foot, rather than your sole. Try to slow the ball down and position it in one smooth movement.

USING YOUR INSTEP

If you use your instep to control the ball, you will be in a good position to play the ball away when you have trapped it.

This player is balanced and in line with the ball.

Make sure you work on receiving with your left and your right foot.

Watch the ball as it approaches and place your foot in line with it. Balance on one leg with your receiving foot turned out.

As you receive the ball with your instep, relax your leg and foot so that they travel back with it, absorbing its speed.

The ball should drop just in front of your feet. Look around you and play it away to the left or right as quickly as possible.

USING THE OUTSIDE OF YOUR FOOT

If you are going to use the outside of your foot, decide to do so quickly and turn so that your side faces the ball.

Lift your leg to receive the ball with the outside of your foot. Relax your foot back and down to the ground.

Push the ball to the outside with the same foot, as you can see here, or across your body with either foot.

USING THE TOP OF YOUR FOOT

To control the ball with the top of your foot, make sure you are facing the ball with your arms out for balance.

Lift your foot, but keep it flat. If you point your toes up the ball will probably bounce off them.

Just as you receive the ball, lower your foot to the ground, letting the ball drop off it in front of you.

THINGS TO AVOID

Try not to stop the ball dead. If you do, you have to touch it again before you can play your next move.

If the ball bounces off your foot and ends up a long way from you, you waste time chasing it.

PASS AND CONTROL EXERCISE

Do this exercise with a friend. Make a 'gate' with two markers and stand with the gate between you. Pass the ball through the gate so that your partner has to control it.

He turns and passes the ball down the outside of the gate. Control it, turn and pass it back through the gate or down the other side of it. Carry on passing and receiving like this.

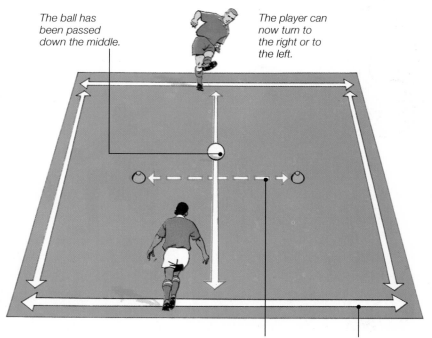

The ball has been passed down the middle.

The player can now turn to the right or to the left.

Try to vary your passes as much as possible, but keep them low.

Anticipate which way the ball will come and run for it.

The gate is about 2m (6ft) wide.

Your field is about 5m (16ft) wide.

HIGHER BALLS

When a ball comes at you from a higher angle, there are several things you can do. Depending on where you position yourself and how high the ball is, you can receive it with your foot, thigh or chest. Whichever you decide upon, you still use a trapping technique to take the pace out of the ball.

USING YOUR THIGH

If you trap the ball properly it shouldn't sting your leg.

Watch the ball carefully so that you can judge where it will land.

Bend your knee to meet the ball, using your arms for balance. On making contact, straighten your leg gradually so that the ball drops off your thigh in front of your feet.

USING YOUR FOOT

Keeping your arms out for balance, lift your leg to meet the ball. Catch it with the instep of your foot.

Without hooking your foot completely under the ball, drop it down to the ground, dragging the ball down with it.

USING YOUR CHEST

Your chest is good for trapping because it is bigger than any other part of your body. Keep your hands open, because clenching your fist makes your chest muscles tighten and they need to relax. Keep your arms out of the way, too, to avoid handling the ball.

Put your arms back and open up your chest as the ball approaches you.

As the ball makes contact with you, trap it by letting yourself relax.

Bring your shoulders in and hollow your chest, so that the ball rolls off you.

The ball drops to the ground gently and you are able to play your next move.

HIGH BALL PRACTICE

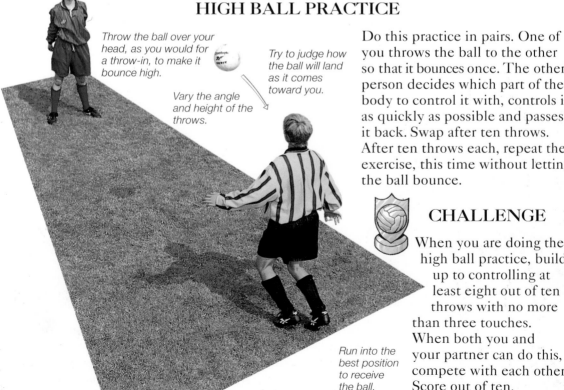

Throw the ball over your head, as you would for a throw-in, to make it bounce high.

Try to judge how the ball will land as it comes toward you.

Vary the angle and height of the throws.

Run into the best position to receive the ball.

Do this practice in pairs. One of you throws the ball to the other so that it bounces once. The other person decides which part of the body to control it with, controls it as quickly as possible and passes it back. Swap after ten throws. After ten throws each, repeat the exercise, this time without letting the ball bounce.

CHALLENGE

When you are doing the high ball practice, build up to controlling at least eight out of ten throws with no more than three touches. When both you and your partner can do this, compete with each other. Score out of ten.

HEADING THE BALL

Controlling the ball with your head is not very easy until you are sure of your heading technique, so these pages show you how to develop a range of heading skills. The main points to remember are to keep your eyes open and to use your forehead, not the top of your head. You may find it easier to begin with a fairly light, soft ball.

BASIC HEADING TECHNIQUE

Put yourself in line with the ball. With one foot in front of the other, bend your knees and lean back.

As the ball comes close, try to keep your eyes open. Stay relaxed right up to the last minute.

Attack the ball with your forehead. If you use any other part of your head it can be painful.

Push the ball away, keeping your neck muscles firm so that your head can direct the ball.

POWER HEADING

Put one foot in front of the other for balance and bend your legs as the ball comes toward you.

Keep your eyes fixed on the ball and take off on one foot. This gives you more power and height.

Drive forward as powerfully as you can with your forehead, keeping your eyes open.

Watch where the ball goes as you land so that you are ready to carry out your next move.

CONTROL HEADING

Use a control header to trap the ball if you want to play the next move yourself instead of passing.

Don't lean quite as far back as the ball approaches. Stay relaxed to provide a cushion for the ball.

Hold your position as you receive the ball. Bend your knees and lean back slightly farther.

Push the ball forward gently, so that it drops and lands not far from your feet.

HEADING PRACTICE

Work with a partner. Stand about 4m (13ft) apart. Your partner throws the ball for you to head back. Have five tries at each of these techniques, then switch.

First, trap the ball with a control header. Let it drop to the ground. Pass it back.

Next, head the ball so that your partner can catch it easily.

Finally, power the ball away, heading it over your partner.

CHALLENGE

Set distance targets. For power headers, try to head the ball more than 6m (20ft). For control headers, try to head it no more than 1m (3ft) from your feet.

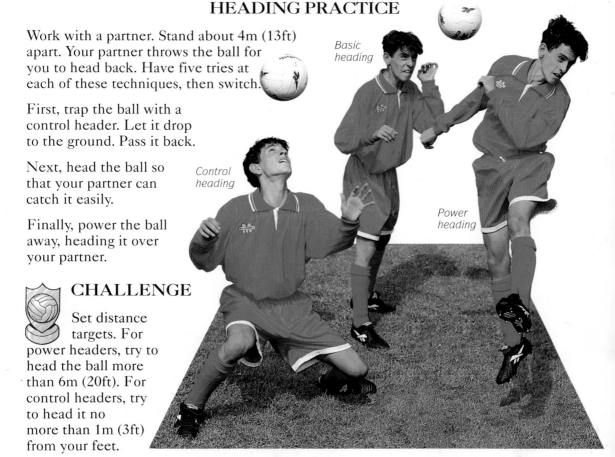

Basic heading

Control heading

Power heading

TURNING

Once you have received the ball and controlled it, you need to move off with it as fast as possible before an opponent can challenge you. You improve your chances of doing this effectively if you can turn quickly and sharply, so it is worth learning several turns to outwit your opponents.

Marker

TURNING 'OFF-LINE'

When you receive the ball, always try to turn immediately and take it off in another direction. This is what is meant by taking the ball 'off-line'. If you keep running in the same direction, it is too easy for your opponents to guess where the ball will go next. They will quickly be able to reach you and tackle you.

The ball has been passed to a player who is being closely marked.

This line shows the 'on-line' route that the player must try to avoid taking.

Instead of taking the on-line route, the player reaches the ball and turns off-line.

DOING AN INSIDE HOOK

As you receive the ball, watch out for approaching opponents and lean in the direction you want to go.

Drop your shoulder so that you are partly turned. Hook the instep of your foot around the ball.

Move off at a sharp angle, dragging the ball around with the inside of your foot. Accelerate away.

DOING AN OUTSIDE HOOK

To begin the turn, reach across your body and hook the ball at the bottom with the outside of your foot.

Sweep the ball around to the side with the same foot. Lean in the direction you want to go.

Turn to follow the path of the ball and accelerate away from your opponent as quickly as possible.

CONTROL AND TURNING EXERCISE

This exercise helps you to develop the different skills of controlling the ball and turning with it into one smooth movement. You will need three or more people.

1. Mark out a circle 10m (33ft) wide. Number the players. The highest (Player 4 here) has the ball and the lowest stands in the middle.

2. Player 4 begins the game by passing the ball into the middle. Player 1 controls it and turns with it. He can turn in any direction.

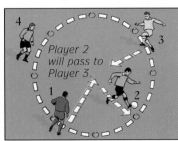

Player 2 will pass to Player 3.

3. Player 1 dribbles the ball to the edge of the circle and Player 2 runs to the middle. Player 1 turns and passes the ball back to Player 2.

4. Player 2 controls the ball, turns and runs to the edge. Player 3 takes his place in the middle. After Player 3, Player 4 runs in, and so on.

STAR TURN

Here, Swiss player Georges Bregy uses an inside hook to pull the ball away from Leonel Alvarez (Columbia).

CHALLENGE

Touching the ball lots of times slows you down, so try to touch it as little as possible. Count the number of touches you need to control the ball and turn it, then reduce this number to four or less.

SPECIAL TURNS

Basic turns are useful for speed, but they do not disguise your movements very much. In many situations, a slightly more complicated turn can help you to fool your opponents. Be flexible, and experiment. You may prefer to develop your own way of doing a particular turn.

THE DRAG BACK TURN

This turn is ideal if you are being closely marked. Once you have mastered it, you can adapt it, depending on your position or that of your opponent.

Think about where to go next.

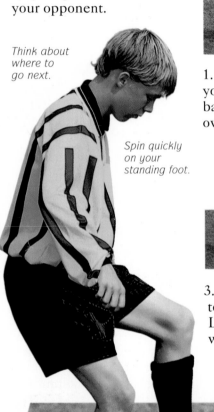

Spin quickly on your standing foot.

1. Draw your leg back as if you are about to kick the ball, but swing your foot over it instead.

2. As you bring your leg back again, catch the top of the ball with your foot and drag it back.

3. As you drag back, begin to spin on your other foot. Lean in the direction you want to go.

4. When you have pulled the ball all the way back, complete the turn. Accelerate past your opponent.

VARIATIONS

Instead of dragging the ball back, step to the inside. Push it away with the outside of your foot.

You can also step to the outside of the ball. Turn, pushing the ball with the instep of your foot.

THE CRUYFF TURN

This turn was named after the Dutch player Johan Cruyff. Try to exaggerate the movements. You can give the turn extra disguise by pretending to kick the ball first.

As you are about to do the turn, swing one foot around the ball so that it is in front of it. Keep this foot firmly on the ground.

Leaning away from the ball, push it back and then behind you with the other foot. Turn quickly and follow the ball.

Try to develop a quick flick of your foot to push the ball around.

Watch where the ball goes so that you can follow it.

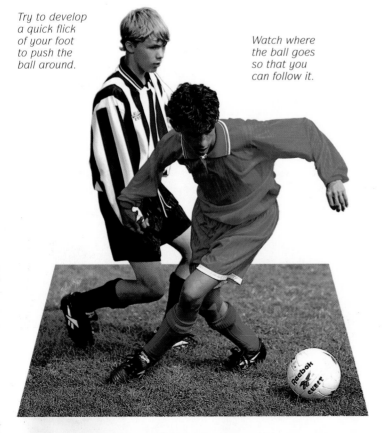

TURNING PRACTICE

Work with a partner. Place four markers in the pattern shown and stand at the end ones. One person is the leader and the other person mirrors what he does.

Both dribble to the middle. Just before the marker, the leader turns. The other tries to mirror his turn.

Run out to the side marker, around it and back to the end ones. Try not to bump into each other as you cross.

Start toward the middle again and turn at the marker. The leader will now be the other player.

CHALLENGE

Compete with each other. Score a point for mirroring a turn correctly, or for fooling your opponent with a turn. Race back to your markers and score a point for winning. The first to ten points wins.

DRIBBLING

Once you have possession of the ball, you may want to pass or shoot, but one of the most exciting parts of playing soccer is keeping the ball under your control and dribbling it up the field. If you watch a good dribbler, the ball seems almost stuck to his feet as he runs. This is what you should aim for.

BASIC TECHNIQUE

You can use your laces to dribble, especially for the first few touches. Be careful not to kick the ball very far.

You are free to run faster if you use the outside of your foot, but try not to tap the ball too far out to the side.

The instep of your foot may feel the most comfortable to use.

Be careful not to let the ball get under your feet.

MOVEMENT AND BALANCE

You need to be flexible and balanced to dribble well. To develop these skills, dribble around a 'slalom' course. Lay ten markers about 4m (13ft) apart in a zigzag line. Start dribbling down the line, weaving around the markers.

4m (13ft)

Try dribbling with different parts of your feet to see which feels most comfortable.

Keep the ball close to your feet. Try to exaggerate the twists and turns, leaning as far as you can as you run.

Keep as close to the path of the slalom as possible. Turn sharply at the markers.

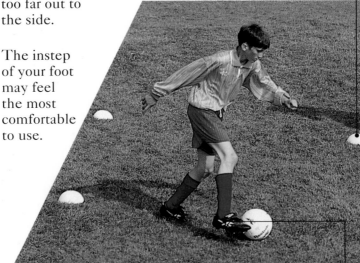

In a game, you would need to look out for other players, so try to look around as you dribble.

Gradually increase your speed. If you find that you cannot lean as far, slow down again until you improve.

Try to run lightly on your toes, so that you can change direction quickly and easily.

TAG DRIBBLE

This game is for up to four people, though more people can play if you make the square bigger.

1. Lay out a 6 x 6m (20 x 20ft) square with four markers. Each player has a ball and stands in the square.

2. Dribble around the square. Try to 'tag' other players without being tagged yourself and without losing control of the ball.

3. Keep a score. You gain a point each time you tag someone, and if you are tagged, you lose a point.

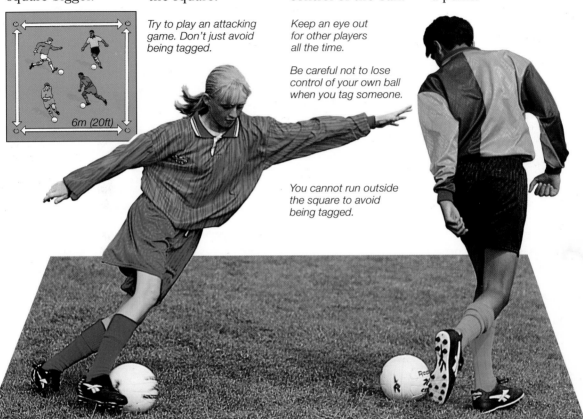

Try to play an attacking game. Don't just avoid being tagged.

Keep an eye out for other players all the time.

Be careful not to lose control of your own ball when you tag someone.

You cannot run outside the square to avoid being tagged.

6m (20ft)

IDEAL TECHNIQUE

Good dribbling should combine tight control with freedom of movement. Some people think that you should dribble with the outside of your foot as much as possible, because it gives you freedom to run and makes it easier for you to turn to the outside.

Here you can see Roberto Baggio of Italy dribbling with the ball at an ideal distance from his feet.

CHALLENGE

The best way to measure how you improve at dribbling is by timing yourself. When you dribble down a slalom, time yourself, then try to beat your record. Try to keep the ball close to your feet. Remember that there is no point in going faster unless the ball is under your control.

WORKING ON PACE

One of the things which will make your dribbling skills more effective is being able to vary your speed. If you can slow down or sprint away suddenly without losing control of the ball, you add disguise to your game and increase your chances of keeping possession.

CHANGES OF PACE

Keep an eye out for opponents and opportunities to pass.

Be ready to slow down and do something different if someone challenges you.

Take long strides so that you cover as much ground as possible.

1. Fool opponents by slowing down. This gives you time to take them by surprise.

2. To dodge around someone, watch for an opportunity to change pace suddenly.

Use the outside of your foot to push the ball forward with little taps.

3. Sprint as fast as possible when you have just dodged around your opponent.

4. When you are clear of opponents, choose the pace that gives you most control.

RUNNING WITH THE BALL

Running with the ball is different from dribbling. It means sprinting up the field with a clear path ahead, pushing the ball a long way in front of you. When you dribble you keep the ball under closer control, beating opponents as you go.

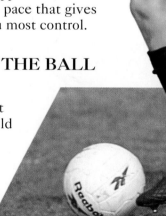

SLALOM AND SPRINT

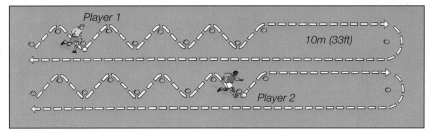

Player 1

10m (33ft)

Player 2

You can play this with as many people as you like. You each need a ball. Lay down ten markers in a zigzag line (see page 14), then place an extra marker 10m (33ft) from the last one. Make one course like this for each person.

At the shout of 'Go!', everyone starts to dribble in and out of the slalom.

At the end of the slalom, accelerate. Run with the ball to the last marker.

Turn, then race back to the starting point with the ball. The first one back wins.

SPRINT AND STOP GAME

This game is for three or more players. Lay out a circle about 3m (10ft) wide and a bigger circle around it. There should be about 10m (33ft) between them. All of you begin to dribble around the inside circle.

Take turns shouting 'Go!' The player who shouts has an unfair advantage, so he cannot be the winner of that game.

To keep the ball close to the circle, use the outside of your foot. Brush the ball along with the foot nearest the circle.

This player has reached the outer circle and stopped with his foot on the ball, so he wins.

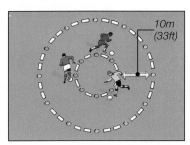

10m (33ft)

On the shout of 'Go!', turn and sprint out from the circle. The first person to reach the outer circle and put a foot on their ball is the winner. Dribble back to the inner circle and start the game again.

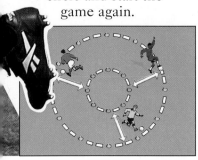

FAKING

Faking means fooling your opponents into going the wrong way while you are dribbling. Two things will make your opponent move in a particular direction, either the movement of your body or the movement of the ball. Faking uses the movement of your body.

A SIMPLE FAKE

The simplest fake is when you pretend to go one way, then swerve and go the other. Here, Player 1 dribbles up the field as Player 2 comes to challenge him.

Player 1

Player 2

Player 1 drops his right shoulder, making Player 2 think that he is going to turn to the right.

Player 2 moves to the right, but Player 1 now swerves back to the left. He dodges around Player 2 and accelerates past him.

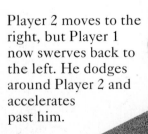

KEY FACTORS

Exaggerate your dropped shoulder and body swerve to fool your opponent.

Accelerate past your opponent before he has time to recover.

Be confident when you try to fake someone, or you risk losing the ball.

A STAR FAKE

Here, Alberto Garcia Aspe of Mexico drops his shoulder to fake Paul McGrath of Ireland.

BASIC FAKING PRACTICE

Work with a partner. Try to dribble past him, using a fake – you are not allowed to just push the ball past him and run.

If you get past him, turn and try again. If you don't, he dribbles past you instead. Score a point each time you get past.

GUESS AND DODGE GAME

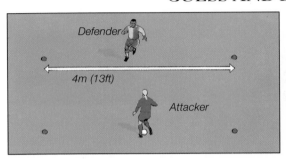

Defender

4m (13ft)

Attacker

The attacker here dodges to the left.

This makes the defender also turn to the left.

1. This is a game for two people with one ball. Both of you stand between two markers placed about 4m (13ft) apart.

2. Decide who will attack and who will defend. The attacker has the ball. The goal is for the attacker to reach a marker.

3. If the defender has his foot on one marker, the attacker has to go the other way. He cannot touch the matching marker.

4. Keep on playing until the attacker reaches a marker, then switch roles so that you both have a turn at being attacker.

A good defender tries to watch the ball, not your movements. This game helps you to develop the speed and anticipation you need to beat him.

You need to be able to switch your balance from one foot to the other.

Once you see that your opponent is off balance, run for your marker quickly.

Here, the attacker has quickly turned to the right to reach the other marker.

FAKING FEATS

If you are trying to fake an opponent while you are dribbling, you stand a better chance of succeeding if you know a few stunt moves. On these pages there are different ways to change direction and unbalance your opponent, which you can use as part of your faking technique.

THE STOP MOVE

1. This move relies on a change of pace. Use it if someone is chasing you.

2. Accelerate slightly. As your opponent speeds up to follow, stop suddenly.

3. You should now be in a good position to use a drag back turn (see page 14).

4. You will be able to carry out the turn while your opponent is still off balance.

5. Finish the turn and start to move away at right angles to your original direction.

6. Your opponent is now facing the wrong way to chase you as you speed off.

THE STOP-START GAME

20m (66ft)

Work with a partner. Mark out a line about 20m (66ft) long. Dribble along it with your partner behind you.

Your partner can come alongside, but he cannot overtake you. Try to 'lose' him by stopping suddenly.

Your partner is thrown off balance.

You may confuse him more if you pretend to stop, then accelerate. Keep the ball on the side farthest from him.

CHALLENGE

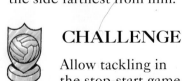

Allow tackling in the stop-start game. Overtaking and sliding tackles are not allowed, but you can try to hook the ball away from the side. Score a point each time you succeed.

THE ZIGZAG MOVE

Try to exaggerate the move.

You don't need to rush.

1. Drop your shoulder and lean left to make it look as though you will push the ball across your body that way.

2. As your opponent gets closer, 'show' him the ball. This confuses him into thinking he can intercept it.

You can reverse this move and turn to the left.

3. Just before he tries to tackle you, slide your right foot around the ball and hook it with the outside of your foot.

4. Pull the ball away to the right and push it past your opponent. Turn to follow it quickly and accelerate away.

SOLO PRACTICE

To gain confidence in using these moves, try doing them on your own with a marker. Pretend the marker is one of your opponents and dodge past it when you get close to it. Try using different moves.

THE SCISSORS MOVE

Dribble forward with the outside of your right foot. Make it look as though you will swerve out to the right.

Lift your foot suddenly and swing it around the front of the ball, taking a big stride as you do so.

Hook the outside of your other foot around the ball. Push it away as fast as you can to the left.

SHIELDING THE BALL

Shielding is a way of keeping control of the ball by preventing other players from getting at it. It is also known as 'screening'. You position yourself so that you become a shield between your opponent and the ball. Try to develop the habit of shielding whenever an opponent challenges you.

HOW TO SHIELD

As soon as you are challenged, turn so that you are between the ball and your opponent.

The ball is now protected. Your opponent can only reach it from behind.

The challenger risks committing a foul if he kicks at the ball from behind. He may kick you accidentally instead.

Keep the ball close to your feet.

The challenger has to try to get in front of you. This gives you time to pass the ball or accelerate away.

SHIELDING WHILE YOU ARE RUNNING

When you are running with the ball or dribbling, keep your head up to watch out for opponents coming up on your left or right side.

Be ready to change your body position from one side of the ball to the other. For example, if someone is coming up on the right, keep the ball on your left side.

IMPEDING OTHER PLAYERS

One of the laws of soccer is that you cannot 'impede the progress' of another player. This means that you cannot stop someone from reaching the ball unless you can play it yourself, or shield another player from the ball while you are still running for it. You cannot push or hold anyone either, so be careful to use your arms only as a shield.

TRUCK AND TRAILER

The trailer is not allowed to tackle.

Play this game in pairs. The player with the ball is the 'truck'. The other is the 'trailer'. The truck dribbles the ball while the trailer tries to get in front of him.

This player is not breaking the rules, as he has possession of the ball. He is using his body and arms as a shield, but he is not holding or pushing the other player.

Here, the player is impeding. He has not yet reached the ball and is holding the other player back. He is also pushing with his arms, which is not allowed.

The truck has to twist and turn so that he is always shielding the ball. When the trailer gets in front of the truck, he becomes the truck instead.

A STAR SHIELDING

Some players are known for shielding the ball more than others. It is important not to be afraid of making physical contact while you are playing, but this never excuses committing a foul.

Here you can see Dutch player Dennis Bergkamp using his arms and body correctly to shield the ball from an opponent.

CHALLENGE

When you are the trailer, make a real effort to dodge around the truck. If you are the truck, try to protect the ball successfully for at least one minute before losing control of it.

SKILLS FOR FUN

Learning extra skills can give your game a lot of flair and disguise. Some of the moves on these pages are just for fun but others add an extra element to your control and dribbling skills, too. Learning any of them is worth the effort because you are still improving your control of the ball.

THE BEARDSLEY TRICK

This trick uses your faking skill. When an opponent comes near, decide quickly on a pretend direction.

Lift your knee in the pretend direction. Really exaggerate the twist of your hips and body.

Your opponent will probably start to go the wrong way. Quickly bring your knee back down.

Before he recovers, push the ball across your body in the opposite direction. Accelerate away.

THE MARADONA MOVE

This move is sure to confuse your opponent. As the ball rolls toward you, step on it to stop it.

Step off the ball again, taking a big stride around it so that you begin to turn around the ball.

Finish turning so that your back is facing the direction you want to go. Put your other foot on top of the ball.

Drag the ball back behind you and quickly spin around again to follow it. Accelerate away.

THE FLICK OVER

This juggling move is very spectacular, but don't use it in a game because you are almost certain to give the ball to the other team. Learn it for fun and compete with your friends to see who can flick it highest.

You can try flicking the ball out to the side rather than over you.

Try not to look around at the ball as you do the flick.

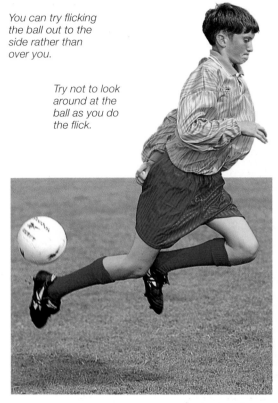

Step in front of the ball with one foot. Trap the ball between the toes of one foot and the heel of your other foot.

Roll the ball up your heel, then flick up backward with your front foot as hard and high as you can so that it goes over you.

THE HEEL CATCH

This is another feat to try while you are juggling. Move in front of the ball, then lean forward and flick your heel up to catch it.

The ball should come around to the front of you again. Spin around to play it back into the air with the top of your foot or knee.

THE NUTMEG

To nutmeg someone you push the ball between his legs. Don't try it unless his legs are far apart. Watch your opponent carefully and time it for when he least expects it. You can then run around him to collect the ball.

PLAYING IN A TEAM

As you build up your control skills, you will find it gradually easier to put them into practice when you are playing in matches. However, when you are playing in a team you need to think carefully about how to make the best use of your skills. Always think of the whole team, not just your own game.

KEEPING POSSESSION

Once your team has possession of the ball, it can control the whole game and create opportunities to score. Whatever you do, you should be helping your team to keep possession. You can do this by remembering these things:

Supporting player

This player is creating a chance to pass.

This player is marking a defender.

This player can see he is in a good position to dribble.

Support your team-mates by backing them up. Let them know you are there by calling to them.

Think ahead. Run into space so that other players can pass to you, or mark an opponent.

If someone passes to you, take the initiative and run for the ball. Don't wait for it to come to you.

When you receive the ball, look around to decide what to do next, then do it as quickly as possible.

DIRECTION

Change direction before opponents can reach you.

This player is passing the ball for his team member to collect.

To support another player, run into space so that he can pass forward to you.

When you are dribbling, it is fine to change direction as long as you are still moving up the field.

If you are being forced to turn back on yourself, you risk wasting time and space. Pass the ball instead.

If you need to pass the ball out of danger, try to pass it forward. Only pass back if you really have to.

WHEN TO DRIBBLE

When you receive the ball, check to see if you are in a good position to dribble. If you are heavily marked but one of your teammates is free, it makes more sense to pass to him. If you try to dribble, you will probably lose possession.

This player is in a better position to play the ball.

Dribbling is safest when the ball is in your opponents' half of the field. Never try to dribble out of your own penalty area, because it is far too risky. Get the ball out of the danger area quickly by passing it up the field instead.

TEAM DUMMIES

Here, the player with the ball can see a supporting player to his right as he dribbles up the field.

When you are dribbling, keep your head up and watch out for other players who are moving with you to give you support.

The player with the ball fakes his opponent and pretends to pass to the right.

When you try to fake an opponent, pretend to pass to a member of your team. This will make your fake more realistic.

As the player with the ball dodges around his opponent, the supporting player moves up with him.

You still have support, so be ready to make a real pass if you come under too much pressure.

IMPROVING CONTROL

To keep on improving, you can play games which develop particular skills. Here, one game helps you to concentrate on your first touch control and the other on your dribbling skills. Try to remember everything you have learned and put it into practice as you play.

TWO TOUCH

'Two touch' is an excellent game for improving your first touch of the ball. It also improves your anticipation, as you have to run into space to play it well.

Make things difficult for the other team by marking closely.

Control the ball with your first touch and pass it with your second.

Mark out a field and two goals. Divide into teams. Play as you would in a normal game, but each player is only allowed to touch the ball twice before another player touches it.

If a player makes a third touch, the ball passes to the other team.

Try this variation if there are five or less of you. Play with just one goal, so that the goalkeeper opposes both teams.

To keep the game moving fast, pass as much as possible before shooting.

REMINDER TIPS

★ Look for space and run into it, so that other players can pass to you.

★ Don't just hope the ball will come directly to you. Run to meet it.

★ Watch the flight of the ball carefully. Get in line with it to receive it.

★ Decide quickly which part of the body you will use to control the ball.

★ Cushion the ball with as few touches as possible. Try to cushion with your first touch.

★ Play your next move quickly before an opponent can reach you.

PINBALL DRIBBLE

This game will help you with your dribbling, faking and shielding skills. Lay out a line of boxes, one for each person playing. In the game shown there are four.

The player in the first box tries to dribble through the next box. The player there tries to tackle him.

If he gets through this box, he scores a point and moves on. He scores a point for each box he dribbles through.

When he loses the ball or gets to the end, he goes into the second box. Everyone else moves back a box.

The player in the last box runs to the first and starts to dribble. Continue playing like this, keeping a note of each player's score. The first person to score five points is the winner.

If the ball goes out of the box, this counts as losing it and the player goes into the second box.

If you find it difficult to get past a particular player, try something different each time you have to pass him.

REMINDER TIPS

★ Keep your head up so that you can see what your opponent is doing.

★ Keep the ball close to you as you dribble, using different parts of your feet.

★ Drop your shoulder and make use of body swerve to fool your opponent.

★ Try out different moves and fakes to unbalance your opponent.

★ Keep your body between the ball and your opponent to shield it from him.

★ Accelerate away from opponents as fast as you can.

WORLD SOCCER QUIZ

Every four years, countries from all over the world compete for the greatest soccer prize of all – the World Cup. Try this quiz to find out how much you know about the history and stars of the World Cup competition. There are questions on other worldwide soccer tournaments as well, including the Olympic Games and the Women's World Championship. The quiz continues on pages 64, 96 and 128, and you can find answers to all the questions on page 128.

1. Which country hosted the first ever World Cup tournament, in 1930?

a. Brazil
b. Uruguay
c. Italy

2. In which American stadium was the 1994 World Cup Final held?

a. Pontiac Silverdome
b. Pasadena Rose Bowl
c. New York Giants Stadium.

3. Which one of these international teams usually plays in red and green?

a. Portugal
b. Croatia
c. Brazil

4. Which player missed the decisive penalty shoot-out kick to put Italy out of the 1994 World Cup Final?

a. Franco Baresi
b. Salvatore Schillaci
c. Roberto Baggio

5. Which country is the only one to have taken part in every World Cup?

a. Brazil
b. Italy
c. France

6. 13 countries took part in the 1930 World Cup. How many entered the 1998 championship?

a. 50-100
b. 100-150
c. over 150

7. Who is the only player to have been in the winning World Cup squad three times?

a. Giuseppe Meazza
b. Pele
c. Roberto Rivelino

8. When was soccer first included in the Olympic Games?

a. 1908
b. 1952
c. 1980

9. Who were the 1995 Women's Soccer World Champions?

a. Norway
b. U.S.A.
c. Germany

10. Which was the last host nation to win the World Cup?

a. England
b. Italy
c. Argentina

11. Which England goalkeeper made the most international appearances?

a. Peter Shilton
b. Gordon Banks
c. David Seaman

12. Who was voted Player of the Tournament in the 1994 World Cup?

a. Roberto Baggio
b. Romario
c. Marco van Basten

13. Mexican goalkeeper Antonio Carbajal played in a record number of World Cups. How many?

a. 3
b. 4
c. 5

14. What was the name of the official mascot for the 1994 World Cup?

a. Ball Boy
b. Striker
c. Stripes

15. Which player was involved in the 'hand of God' incident in the 1986 World Cup in Mexico?

a. Diego Maradona
b. Paul Gascoigne
c. Lothar Matthäus

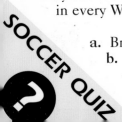
SOCCER QUIZ

PART TWO
PASSING AND SHOOTING

CONTENTS

BEFORE YOU START

This part of the book looks at the kicking, heading and team skills that you need to pass or shoot well. As before, there are plenty of games and exercises to help you improve. Here you can find out about the soccer terms that you'll come across as you read.

PARTS OF THE FOOT

These are the parts of your feet you use most often for passing and shooting. You rarely use your heel or sole.

The **inside** of your foot is from your big toe back to your ankle.

The top of your foot is called the **laces.** It doesn't include your toes.

The **outside** of your foot is from your little toe back to your ankle.

'OVER THE BALL'

Your position 'over the ball' refers to how far forward or back you are leaning. It is important because it affects how powerful and how high your kick will be. If your head is over the ball, your kick is more likely to stay low, and it may be more accurate, too.

This player is well balanced, with his head over the ball.

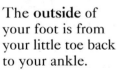

WHERE TO KICK THE BALL

You make the ball go in different directions by knowing which part of it to kick. To figure out which part is which, think of it as having two sides, a top and a bottom. The diagrams below show you how this will be illustrated.

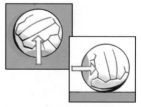

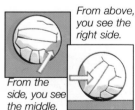

From above, you see the right side.

From the side, you see the middle.

When you are told to kick one side of the ball, you see a diagram of it as it looks from above when you kick. Kick to the left or right.

Diagrams like this show the top or bottom of the ball by looking at it side on, so imagine what it would look like from the side as you kick.

When you are told to kick the ball through the middle, this means both the middle from above and the middle from the side.

If you are told just one part of the ball to kick, for example the right side, you can assume you kick through the middle from the other angle.

BACKSWING AND FOLLOW-THROUGH

Your **backswing** means the action of swinging your leg back before kicking.

Your **follow-through** is when you swing your leg forward and up after kicking.

The backswing

The follow-through

USING BOTH FEET

Just as you need to be able to control the ball with either foot, you need to practise all passing and shooting techniques with both feet. If you can only play well with one foot, you have to waste time moving the ball into a good position before playing it away. This can mean that you miss good chances to pass or shoot.

This left-footed pass sends the ball to the right.

SOCCER TERMS

A handful of special soccer terms are used to describe different parts of the field and particular types of players. The **attacking third** means the third of the field closest to your opponents' goal. The **defending third** is the third of the field closest to your own goal.

This is the red team's defending third.

In this part of the book, an **attacker** is any player in a team which has the ball. A **defender** is any player in a team which doesn't have the ball.

DISGUISE, PACE AND TIMING

Giving a kick **disguise** means making it difficult to guess which way it will go.

The **pace** of the ball is how fast it is going. If a ball 'has pace', it is going fast.

Good **timing** means judging the best time to hit the ball when you pass or shoot.

This is the red team's attacking third and the yellow team's defending third.

INSTEP KICKS

The inside of your foot, or the instep, is the area you use most often for kicking. It has a larger kicking surface than any other part of your foot. This makes it easier for you to judge how the ball will respond when you kick it, so it is ideal for accurate passes.

THE PUSH PASS

This is a low kick for short distances. It is called a pass, but you can use it to shoot at close range. It is easy to learn, and accurate.

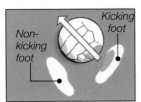

Non-kicking foot
Kicking foot

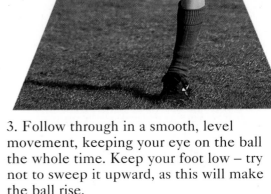

1. Swing your foot back, turning it out so that it is almost at right angles to your other foot.

2. Keep your ankle firm and your body over your feet. Make contact with the middle of the ball.

3. Follow through in a smooth, level movement, keeping your eye on the ball the whole time. Keep your foot low – try not to sweep it upward, as this will make the ball rise.

ACCURACY PRACTICE

Work with a friend. Place two markers 60cm (2ft) apart. One of you stands 1m (3ft) in front of them, the other 1m (3ft) behind. Try to pass to each other through the gap. Score a point for each success.

After five passes each, move another 1m (3ft) apart and start again. Keep going until you are 10m (33ft) apart. The player with the most points wins.

2m (6ft)

HOW TO MEASURE

The measurements for the exercises and games in this section are given in meters (m) and feet (ft). Think of 1m (3ft) as about one big stride. You can then measure out the correct distances easily in strides.

THE INSTEP SWERVE

Swerving the ball is a really useful skill to learn for passing or shooting. You have more control with your instep than the outside of your foot, so it is best to learn the instep swerve first.

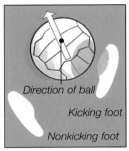

Direction of ball

Kicking foot

Nonkicking foot

The ball should swerve out, then swing back in again.

Follow through freely, your foot rising to follow the direction of the ball.

1. Keep your eyes on the ball as you swing your leg back. Your nonkicking foot should be well out of the way of the ball.

2. Use the side of your foot to kick. The secret is to kick the ball in the right place. (See above).

PIG IN THE MIDDLE

Play this game with two friends. Stand in a line with 10m (33ft) between you. The player in the middle cannot move more than 60cm (2ft) to either side. The players at each end try to bend the ball around the player in the middle. If he is able to intercept it, the player who kicked it takes his place.

Mark out your positions so that you can't cheat.

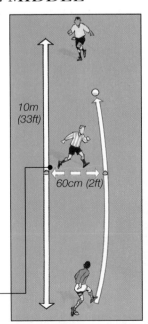

10m (33ft)

60cm (2ft)

STAR PUSH PASS

This picture shows Romanian player Dan Petrescu following through a push pass. See how his foot is still level and low, and how his weight is balanced over his knees.

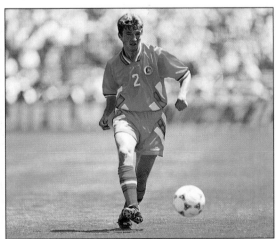

OUTSIDE FOOT KICKS

When you use the outside of your foot to kick the ball, you can disguise your movements very well. Also, because the ball is to one side of you, you are able to move freely and pass or shoot as you run. However, accuracy and control can be difficult, so you will need to practice hard.

FLICKING THE BALL TO THE SIDE

This move is particularly useful when you are under pressure and you receive a fast pass from the side which you do not have time to control. The trick is to let the ball bounce off the outside of your foot, while at the same time directing it to a teammate with a flick of your ankle.

Make contact with little toe area

You don't need any backswing.

1. Keep your back to anyone marking you. Turn the outside of your foot toward the ball.

2. Don't cushion the ball as it makes contact. Direct it out to the side with a flick of your foot.

3. If the ball has been kicked through the middle, it should stay low but fast. Try to direct it into the path of another player.

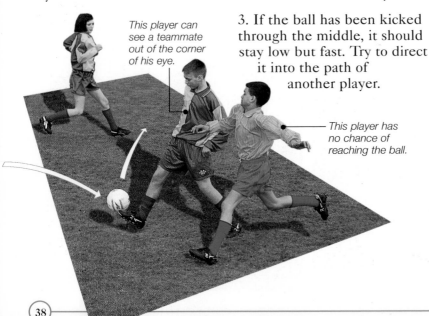

This player can see a teammate out of the corner of his eye.

This player has no chance of reaching the ball.

FLICK GAME

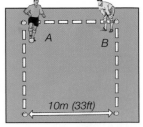

A *B*

10m (33ft)

This is for two players (A and B). Mark out a 10m (33ft) square. Start in the two top corners.

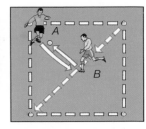

A *B*

B runs across the square as A passes the ball into his path. B returns it with a flick pass.

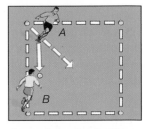

A *B*

A pushes the ball to B, then starts to run. B feeds the ball for him to flick back. Continue like this.

OUTSIDE FOOT SWERVES

This kick makes the ball swerve away to the side. It is a difficult kick to master, and you need to be strong to make it go a long way. However, you don't need to control the ball before you kick it and you can do it as you run, so it is an ideal kick to use for shots at goal.

Hit the ball halfway up if you want it to stay low.

Nonkicking foot

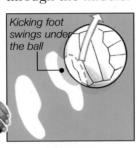

1. Swing your leg back. As you swing your foot back toward the ball, turn the toes of your kicking foot in slightly toward your other foot. Kick the inside of the ball with the area around your little toe.

2. Give the kick plenty of follow-through, sweeping your leg across your body. The ball should swerve out away from you.

Your non-kicking foot should be well out of the way of your kicking foot.

LOFTED SWERVES

A 'lofted' kick means a high kick. If you want an outside foot swerve to go higher and clear other players, kick the ball through its lower half and not through the middle.

Kicking foot swings under the ball

PAIRS PRACTICE

Pass the ball down a straight line. Try to make it swing out from the line and back in again by using outside foot swerves.

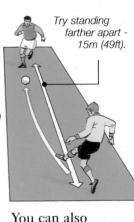

Try standing farther apart - 15m (49ft).

You can also practice outside foot swerves by playing 'Pig in the Middle' (see page 37).

USING YOUR LACES

The top of your foot, or your 'laces', is the area over your shoelaces. It is the most powerful part of your foot, so use it if you want to kick the ball very hard. At first you may accidentally use your toes, but this will improve with practice.

THE LOW LACES DRIVE

You can use this kick as you are running to send it a long way. It is fairly difficult to make it accurate, but the secret of success is to hit the ball right through the middle.

Toes

Nonkicking foot
(alongside ball)

Place your nonkicking foot close to the ball.

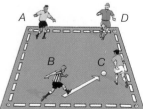

1. Swing your kicking leg well back, so that your heel almost reaches up to your behind.

2. Point your toes toward the ground and make contact with the middle of the ball.

3. Swing your foot onward in the direction of the ball, but make sure your ankle is still stretched out toward the ground as you follow through. This is the key to keeping the kick low.

LACES PASS GAME

Use this game to help you develop your basic laces kicking technique. It is best with four people, but you could play with any number above two – change the shape of the field to make a corner for each player.

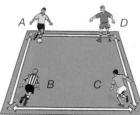

Mark out a 30m (98ft) square. Label yourselves A, B, C and D and stand at its four corners.

A passes to B at an angle so that he has to run to it. B receives it and passes it at an angle to C.

After passing, B stays where he is. C runs to the ball and passes to D, and so on around the square.

THE LOFTED DRIVE

The lofted drive is a long, high kick. The technique for doing it is similar to the technique for low laces kicks, but you kick the ball in a different place and let your foot swing up completely when you follow through.

Kicking the ball on its lower half makes it rise.

1. Approach the ball from a slight angle. Swing your leg back, looking down at the ball as you do so.

2. Make contact with the lower half of the ball, so that the top of your foot reaches slightly under it.

3. Follow through with a sweeping movement, letting your leg swing up across your body.

GAINING POWER AND HEIGHT

You will find that your drives will be higher and more powerful if you lean back as you swing your leg toward the ball. This usually happens naturally, though you may find it easier if you kick from slightly farther away.

This player leans well back, showing his confidence in kicking the ball powerfully.

PERFECTING YOUR TECHNIQUE

To improve your lofted drives you may think you just need to kick the ball harder, but it is more important to develop your technique. In this game you practice drives that need to be accurate as well as powerful to reach their target.

Four of you (A, B, C, D) can work at this by marking out a row of four boxes, all 10m (33ft) square. Each of you stands in a box, which you cannot move out of.

A and B try to lob the ball over C and D. Score a point for each success. If C or D manages to intercept the ball, he takes the place of the player who kicked it.

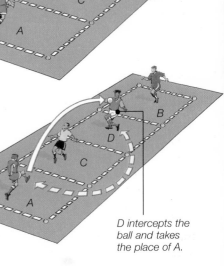

D intercepts the ball and takes the place of A.

VOLLEYING

Volleying means kicking the ball before it has hit the ground. It is a fast and exciting way to play the ball, because you don't spend time controlling it before playing it. This gives the ball pace and makes it harder for your opponents to guess where it is going to go.

FRONT VOLLEY

Front volleys are probably the easiest volleys to do, but you still need quick reactions to do them well. You use the top of your foot to receive the ball, so you need to be facing it. Otherwise, it can be difficult to keep your balance and the volley may go out of control.

Kick through the lower half of the ball.

The ball makes contact with your laces.

LEARNING TO VOLLEY

Work with a friend. Stand 3m (10ft) apart. Drop the ball onto your foot and volley it to him gently for him to catch.

3m (10ft)

VARYING THE HEIGHT

If you make contact later, your nonkicking foot should be closer to the ball.

1. Lift your knee as the ball approaches. Point your toes and stretch out your ankle.

2. As you direct the ball away, try to keep your head forward over your knee.

If you want to send the ball high, perhaps to clear a defender, get your foot right under the ball.

To stop the ball from rising too much, lift your foot up over the ball slightly after making contact.

SIDE VOLLEY

Side volleys are more difficult than front volleys. You need quick reactions, as you do for any volley, but the leg movement that you have to do is also more difficult – you need to be able to balance on one leg while you are leaning sideways.

1. Watch the ball as it comes toward you so that you can judge the right angle to meet it.

2. As you lift your outside leg up, make sure that the shoulder nearest the ball isn't in the way.

3. Swing your leg up and around in a sideways movement so that your laces make contact.

4. Follow through in the direction of the ball by swinging your leg completely across your body.

HIGHER AND LOWER

If you want to keep the ball low, try to make contact with the ball just above the middle.

To make the ball rise over the heads of other players, kick it just below the middle.

SIDE ACTION PRACTICE

Because the leg movement is the most difficult part of this volley, you may find it helps to practice over an obstacle. Make or find something that is almost as high as your hip, and try swinging your leg over it. You can put the ball on top of it if you want. If it is too high to reach, begin with a lower obstacle.

TRIO VOLLEY GAME

When you can do the leg movement, play this with two friends. A throws the ball to B, who volleys to C. C throws the ball for A to volley, and so on.

Score a point each time you volley accurately. The player with the most points after ten volleys each is the winner.

MORE ABOUT VOLLEYING

Much of the skill in volleying depends on having the confidence to strike the ball early. If you take the initiative and go for the ball instead of waiting for it to reach you, you will find it easier to control its direction. All the volleys on these pages are most effective if you act quickly and decisively.

THE HALF-VOLLEY

To do a half-volley, you kick the ball just as it bounces. If you kick it correctly, it should stay low and also be quite powerful. Point your toes, stretch your ankle, then kick the ball with the top of your foot. Your knee should make a firm snapping action.

Once it is kicked, the ball shoots off very fast.

Your nonkicking foot is alongside the ball and a little behind it.

1. Judge the flight of the ball and position yourself just behind where it will land. Take a short backswing.

2. Keeping your head forward so that it is in line with your knee, kick the ball as soon as it hits the ground.

VOLLEYS IN THE AIR

If the ball is very high, you may need to jump for it and volley it in the air.

Use a front or side volley technique, depending on the angle of the ball.

Your timing has to be especially good, so keep your eye on the ball all the time.

Watch the flight of the ball as you land. Get ready to follow the ball forward.

THE 'LAY-OFF' VOLLEY

'Laying the ball off' means playing the ball to another player when you don't have much time to play it yourself. To play a 'lay-off' volley, take the ball early and direct it out to the left or right with your first touch.

Here, a defender is in a position to challenge the player receiving the ball. He can see that a teammate is in a better position to play the ball forward, so he lays it off to him.

Instead of using your laces, turn your foot to use the inside or outside of it.

Make contact with the middle of the ball, or slightly above the middle to send the ball down.

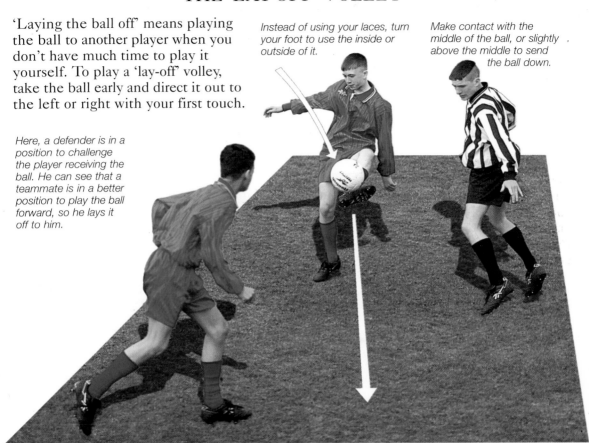

ONE BOUNCE GAME

In this game, you can make use of all the volleys you have learned. It is for three or more players, though it is best with about six. Each player begins with five lives.

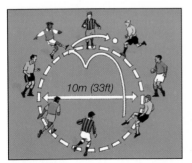

10m (33ft)

Stand in a circle 10m (33ft) across. One player kicks the ball high to another player, who lets it bounce once then volleys it to someone else. Use any type of volley.

You lose a life for missing or mis-hitting a volley. The winner is the last with any lives left. Next, play without letting the ball bounce (apart from half-volleys).

STAR VOLLEY

Here, Alessandro del Piero of Italy jumps for a volley. Even though he is at full speed, he is balanced and has his eye on the ball.

CHIPPING

The chip is a kick which makes the ball rise very quickly into the air. It is not very powerful, but it is ideal for lifting the ball over opponents' heads, especially the goalkeeper's.

Here, the player watches the ball as it rises up away from him.

BASIC TECHNIQUE

The secret of the chip is to stab at the ball without following through. The area just below your laces acts like a wedge which punches the ball into the air.

Direction of ball

1. Face the ball straight on. It is almost impossible to chip from the side. Take a short backswing.

2. Bring your foot down with a sharp stabbing action, aiming your foot at the bottom of the ball.

3. Your foot kicks into the ground as it hits the ball, which is why there is no follow-through. This should happen naturally – it doesn't really matter if your leg does swing up as long as the ball flies into the air.

TECHNIQUE TIPS

Your nonkicking foot should be alongside the ball and close to it, only about 20cm (8in) away.

Kicking foot—

Vary your chips by leaning forward or back. If you lean back, the chip will not fly as high, but it may go farther.

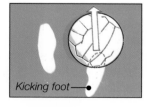

CHIPPING PRACTICE

You can chip the ball when it is still or when it is moving. It is probably easiest to do if you run to the ball as it is moving toward you. This exercise allows you to practice your basic chipping technique with the ball coming toward you.

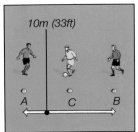

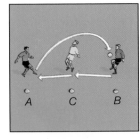

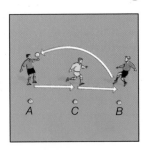

The exercise is for three players. Lay out three markers 10m (33ft) apart.

C passes along the ground to A. A chips it over C to B, who plays it back to C.

C plays the ball along the ground to B, who chips it to A. A passes it to C.

If A or B mis-hits a chip, he goes into the middle and C takes his place.

COMPARING HIGH KICKS

It is difficult to chip very far, so use a lofted drive for longer kicks. Here, you practice both types of kicks. You need two or more players. Divide into two groups. Put six markers in a row, 5m (16ft) apart, and mark out a 5m (16ft) area around each one.

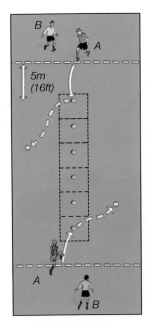

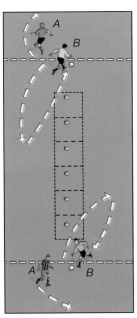

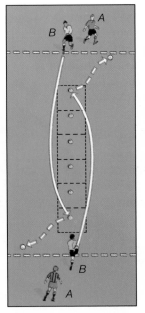

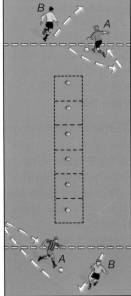

Stand 5m (16ft) from each end of the row. The first player tries to chip into the first area, aiming for the marker in the middle.

Score 10 for hitting the area, 20 for the marker. The next player gets the ball while you go to the back of the line.

All of you try hitting the first area, then move on to the next. Use lofted drives for the last three areas, instead of chips.

To keep from running to get the ball, pick up the opposite group's long drives. Keep playing, making a note of the score.

TRICK MOVES

Sometimes a trick move is just what you need to take your opponents by surprise. Some of them can be fairly risky, though, so only use them in the attacking third of the field where losing the ball does not put your team in too much danger. Some of these tricks are easy to perform and others need quite a bit of practice.

THE BACKHEEL PASS

To do a backheel pass, you kick the ball back with your heel, or sometimes your sole. You can completely surprise your opponents if you do it quickly, and if there is a teammate behind you to receive it.

For a basic backheel pass, keep your foot level as you kick so that it doesn't jab down at the ball.

To get a different angle or to fake your movements, you can cross one leg over the other.

You can roll the ball back with your sole. Point your toes down and kick the middle of the ball.

THE CHEST PASS

Sometimes, when the ball comes at you from a high angle, you have very little time to control it before passing it. You can use your chest to redirect it, but only if the ball is traveling fast – your chest will tend to cushion a slow ball.

Tense your chest muscles and stick your chest out to make a hard surface for the ball to bounce off. Redirect it to a teammate by turning quickly to the left or right as it reaches you.

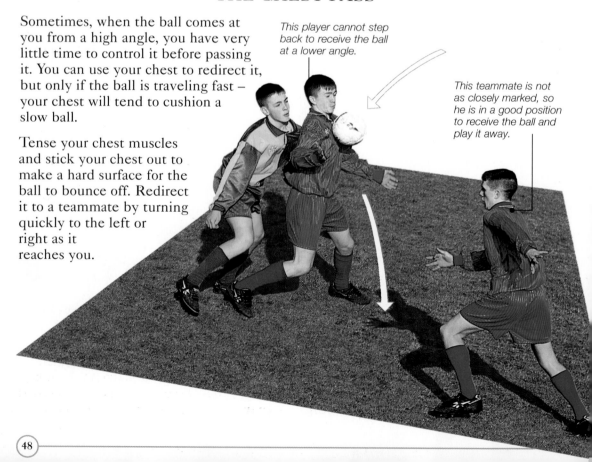

This player cannot step back to receive the ball at a lower angle.

This teammate is not as closely marked, so he is in a good position to receive the ball and play it away.

THE BICYCLE OVERHEAD KICK

This is a spectacular and exciting kick, but it is also very risky. Never try it in the defending third of the field, or in a crowded area where you might kick someone. Also, remember that if you fall you cannot follow up your pass, so make sure other players can follow it up instead.

1. The ball should be at about head height. Take off on one leg, jumping backward.

2. Keep your eye on the ball and swing your kicking foot up over head height.

3. At the highest point of your jump, strike the ball with your laces.

At the highest point of the kick, your foot is at other players' head height. This means you need to be especially careful not to kick someone.

Try to kick the ball through the middle.

4. Cushion your fall by relaxing and rolling on your shoulder. This will stop you from hurting your wrists.

VARIATIONS

If the ball is not quite as high, you can do overhead kicks while keeping your nonkicking foot on the ground. Lift your kicking foot up to reach the ball, keeping your arms out for balance.

If the ball is farther away from you, try the 'scissors' kick. It is a little like the side volley (see page 43), but you jump and kick while you are sideways in the air.

HOW TO PRACTICE

Practice on soft grass or a cushioned mat. Get a friend to help you and stand about 5m (16ft) apart. Your friend throws the ball to you for you to kick.

At first, work on landing safely. Once you are sure about this, work on timing your jump, because timing is the main secret of success.

WHAT MAKES A GOOD PASS?

Good passing is not just about mastering clever passes or trick moves. A good pass has to be useful to your team. This means that you need to look around you and think before you pass, then use a pass that is best for the situation – even if it is the simplest one you know.

ACCURACY

Accurate passing between teammates makes it much more difficult for opponents to intercept the ball. It also saves time, because the player receiving it can take it forward immediately.

This acute angle pass reaches a player on the wing.

Direction is the first key to accuracy. Try to place the ball where it can be easily received by your teammate.

A defender has managed to intercept this short pass.

Pace is important, too. If your pass is too soft an opponent will intercept it. Make sure it is hard enough.

This pass has gone out of play.

Try not to pass the ball too hard, either. If you do, it will be difficult to control and may go too far.

CHOOSING YOUR KICK

There is no such thing as the 'right' kick to use, because each situation is different. However these are some general points to bear in mind before you pass.

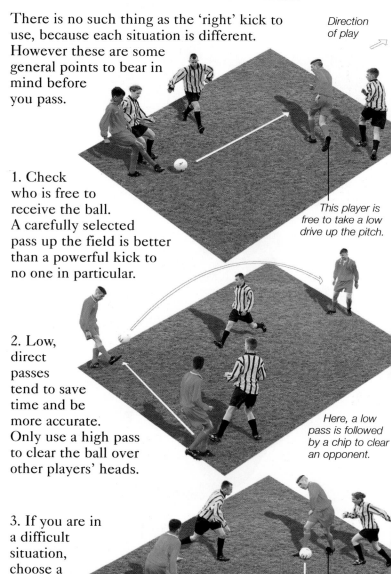

Direction of play

This player is free to take a low drive up the pitch.

Here, a low pass is followed by a chip to clear an opponent.

This player uses a simple push pass.

1. Check who is free to receive the ball. A carefully selected pass up the field is better than a powerful kick to no one in particular.

2. Low, direct passes tend to save time and be more accurate. Only use a high pass to clear the ball over other players' heads.

3. If you are in a difficult situation, choose a pass that you can do easily. This is better than giving the ball away.

FAKING YOUR OPPONENTS

You can create opportunities for your team by distracting or confusing your opponents, and by making it difficult for them to guess where the ball will go.

1. Disguise your intentions by pretending to kick the ball in a different direction before you pass.

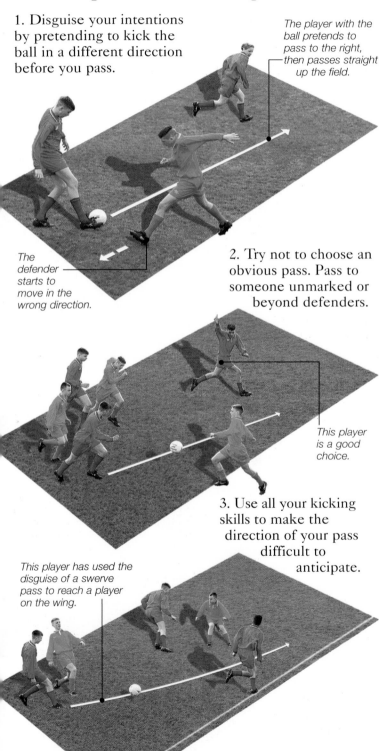

The player with the ball pretends to pass to the right, then passes straight up the field.

The defender starts to move in the wrong direction.

2. Try not to choose an obvious pass. Pass to someone unmarked or beyond defenders.

This player is a good choice.

3. Use all your kicking skills to make the direction of your pass difficult to anticipate.

This player has used the disguise of a swerve pass to reach a player on the wing.

TIMING

Even if you manage to pass accurately, you can miss your teammate altogether if you pass at the wrong time. Also, your teammate is more likely to be able to collect a slightly inaccurate pass if your timing is good.

This player can intercept the pass.

Passing the ball too early gives your opponents the opportunity to run and intercept it.

This defender has caught up with the player in space.

If you wait too long before passing, an opponent may start marking the teammate who was free.

TIPS FOR SUCCESS

★ Practice all the different kicks so that you are confident enough to try any of them.

★ Look around you as you play so that you can make the best use of any opportunities to pass.

★ Communicate with your teammates. Shout to each other or use hand signals to attract attention.

PASSING TACTICS

Tactics can mean the special team formations that you plan out before a game. They can also be the moves and decisions you make because of the position you are in on the field, or the ways that you work with other players to get the ball away from your opponents.

PLAYING IN DEFENSE

As a defender, your prioritiy is keeping the ball out of danger. This often means passing it forward, using long drives and volleys to send the ball up the field or over attackers' heads.

Defender A has two options. He can pass forward to B or across to C. He chooses to pass to B, which is the best thing to do. If he had passed to C, the ball would not be any farther up the field.

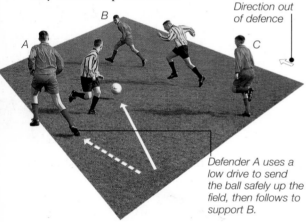

Direction out of defence

Defender A uses a low drive to send the ball safely up the field, then follows to support B.

A good defender only passes the ball back when he has no alternative. Here, A is surrounded. He passes back to a supporting player (B) who is in a better position to play the ball up the field to C.

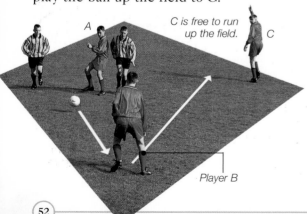

C is free to run up the field.

Player B

ATTACKING PLAY

If you are playing farther up the field, you can take more risks. You need to play quickly to confuse defenders, using all the tricks and different passes possible to cut a path through to the goal.

Direction of play

Here, very rapid play using short push passes and volleys gets the ball past defenders.

Play in the middle of the field can get very cramped. Spread the play by passing out to the wing.

Try to pass the ball beyond defenders, especially to players who are in a good position to shoot.

Take defenders by surprise by turning to pass the ball in an unexpected direction or difficult angle.

GIVE AND GO PASSES

Give and go passes are also known as wall passes. Just before an opponent tackles you, pass the ball quickly to a teammate, then run around your opponent before he has time to recover. Your teammate acts as a 'wall'. He passes the ball back to you quickly and you take it forwards up the field.

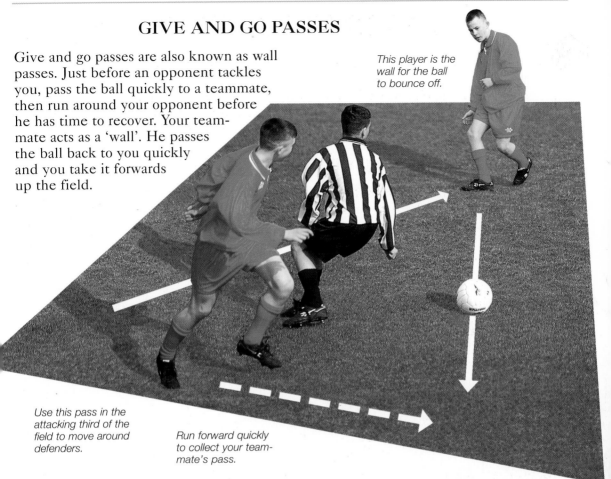

This player is the wall for the ball to bounce off.

Use this pass in the attacking third of the field to move around defenders.

Run forward quickly to collect your teammate's pass.

CROSSOVER PLAYS

This tactic uses a short outside foot pass to do two things. You bring two opponents together, creating space for your own team. You also change the path of the ball before they realize what you have done.

A and B can now move out to the wings.

Player A and Player B are both being marked. Player A has the ball. A and B run toward each other, taking their markers with them.

As they cross each other, A quickly passes the ball to B with the outside of his foot. The markers are confused and get left behind.

THINKING AHEAD

In order to make your team's tactics effective, keep thinking ahead. Check the position of players around you to figure out what they will do next. This will help you to decide what to do, too.

Here, Portugal's Luis Figo has escaped Neil Lennon of Northern Ireland, and is looking up to figure out his next move.

SUPPORT PLAY

Supporting means helping your teammates when you don't have the ball yourself. Each player only has the ball for a small part of each soccer match, so what he does for the rest of the time is very important for his team's success.

FINDING SPACE

Another term for finding space is 'running off the ball'. It means escaping opponents and getting into an open space so that teammates can pass to you. Opponents may soon catch up, so you need to keep moving into different positions.

It can be tempting to run toward the ball even if a teammate has it. Try not to do this. Think about where he could pass to, and run there instead.

DECOY RUNS

A 'decoy run' means running into a good position, but then not receiving a pass. It is a way of fooling opponents into running away from the ball.

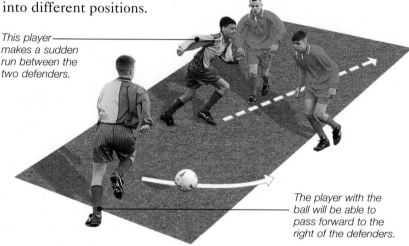

This player makes a sudden run between the two defenders.

The player with the ball will be able to pass forward to the right of the defenders.

One kind of decoy move is making your marker think you are about to receive the ball, then letting it run on to a teammate.

CREATING GOOD ANGLES

'Creating a good angle' refers to how useful your supporting position is. A good angle is one where your teammate can see you and where you are in a good position for him to pass to.

Direction of play

Here, the player runs for a forward pass.

This player runs down the wing. His teammate reaches him with a wide-angled pass.

This defender is drawn away from the ball by a decoy run.

Always try to place yourself where your teammate can pass forward, not across.

A wide-angled pass is less easy to predict, and is more likely to split your opponents' defense.

Another decoy move is turning away from the ball, taking a defender with you, so that your teammate can run forward.

'PASS AND MOVE'

It is always exciting when you have possession of the ball. However, as soon as you pass it on to another player, you need to start supporting again right away. Always move to follow up your pass, or to find another good supporting position.

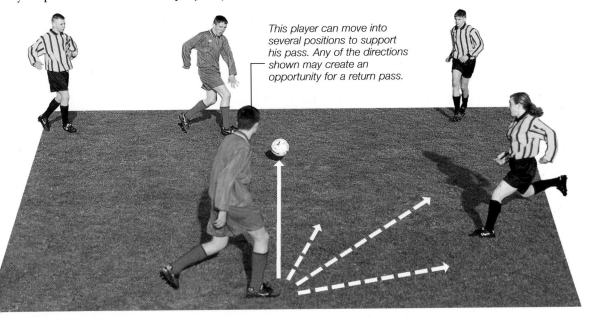

This player can move into several positions to support his pass. Any of the directions shown may create an opportunity for a return pass.

PASS AND MOVE EXERCISE

This exercise helps you to get into the habit of following up your passes. You need three or more players. Divide up into two opposite rows.

The first player in one row passes to the first in the other, then runs to the end of the opposite row.

The player at the front of that row passes back and follows the ball. Continue like this.

SUPPORT GAME

This game is best played by seven players, two defenders (labeled D) and five attackers (A). As you play, use the support skills that you have learned. Run off the ball to find space, work out the best kick to use before passing and follow up your passes.

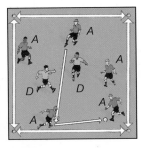

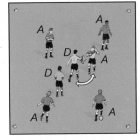

Mark out a pitch about 20m (66ft) square. You need one ball. The As have the ball and try to pass to each other without the Ds intercepting.

If a D manages to intercept, he swaps places with the A player who passed. If the As manage ten passes in a row, the Ds swap with two As anyway.

HEADING IN ATTACK

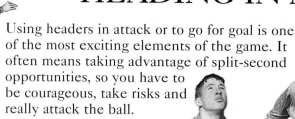

Using headers in attack or to go for goal is one of the most exciting elements of the game. It often means taking advantage of split-second opportunities, so you have to be courageous, take risks and really attack the ball.

DOWNWARD HEADERS

When heading for goal, you should try to keep the ball down to make it more difficult for goalkeepers to save. To make the ball go down when you head it, you need to get above it to hit the top part of it, then nod your head down firmly as you make contact.

1. To catch the top part of the ball with your forehead, you often have to jump.

2. As you would for any header, try to keep your eyes open all the time.

3. As you head the ball away, push forward and down with your forehead.

DIVING HEADERS

Usually, you use a diving header to try for goal. This is a very dramatic way of scoring, but bear in mind that once you have committed yourself you will be on the ground and unable to play another move until you get up again.

This player watches where the ball has gone. He must now get up quickly in case he needs to follow it up.

Approach a diving header with plenty of speed. This will add to its power.

Keep your eyes on the ball and dive forward, letting your legs leave the ground.

Direct the ball to the left or right by turning your head as you make contact.

As you hit the ground, try to relax your body so that you don't hurt yourself.

HEADING PRACTICE

This is a practice for three players. Mark out a goal 6m (20ft) across. Place a marker 15m (49ft) in front of it. One player is the goalkeeper.

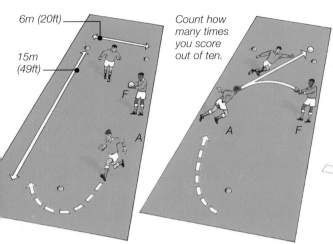

6m (20ft)

15m (49ft)

Count how many times you score out of ten.

One player (F) stands at the side of the goal. The other (A) stands between the goal and the marker. A runs around the marker as F throws the ball to him.

A has to rush for the ball and head at goal. F should vary the height of the ball for A to try different headers. Rotate players after ten turns.

FLICK-ON HEADERS

There is one exception to the rule of using your forehead when heading, and that is when you let the ball glance off the top of your head. You usually do this to lift the ball out of the reach of a defender, to a teammate who may be able to shoot.

As the ball passes over you, jump straight into the air and let it glance off your head. It continues in basically the same direction, though you can direct it left or right slightly.

THROW-HEAD-CATCH GAME

This game is for eight or more players. Divide into two teams. Each team has a goal and goalkeeper. Everyone else marks a player from the other team. To play, you must follow the sequence 'throw, head, catch', even when you intercept the ball. You can only score a goal with a header.

SHOOTING TO SCORE

Once you have mastered all the different kicking techniques and passing skills, you have all the basic skills that you need for shooting, too. However there are several things to bear in mind which can make a big difference to the number of goals you score.

WHAT WILL HELP YOU TO SCORE?

Try to keep the ball low. It is easier for a goalkeeper to stretch for a high ball than to reach down for a low one.

Aim at the far corners of the goal. The goalkeeper can more easily save shots which come straight at him.

Vary your approach to goal. If you always take the same approach, defenders will be likely to intercept you.

Shoot whenever you have the chance. Go for risky shots. It's better to take a shot and miss than not to take a shot at all.

Try not to look in the direction you are going to shoot. This makes your shot too easy to anticipate.

Practice shooting from an sharp angle. Angled shots are difficult to anticipate and to save.

ACCURACY

You may think you need power to be shoot effectively. It is true that hard shots are difficult to save, but they are also difficult to control. There is no point in a hard shot if you miss, so it is better to work on your accuracy first.

REBOUND SHOTS

When you shoot, don't stop to see what happens. The ball may hit the post, or the goalkeeper may drop the ball.

If you keep moving and follow your shot in toward the goal, you can shoot again if the ball rebounds.

WHEN NOT TO SHOOT

Whenever you can see a clear path to goal you should try a shot. Sometimes, though, it's not so clear and a teammate may have a better chance of scoring than you. Then, it is better to pass than to shoot.

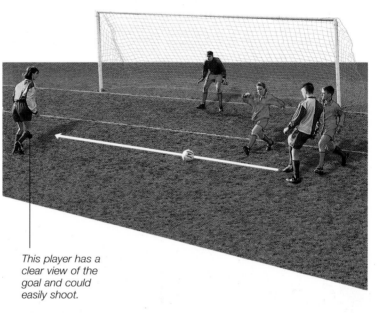

This player has a clear view of the goal and could easily shoot.

TARGET PRACTICE

The best way to improve your shooting is to practice aiming at a target. You can do this by marking a target on a wall to shoot at, but it is even better to practice against a goalkeeper. This exercise is for five players. It should improve your speed and accuracy.

15m (49ft)

6m (20ft)

15m (49ft)

Keep the shots as low as possible.

Aim for the corners of the goal.

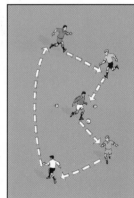

Mark out a goal 6m (20ft) wide. Stand in pairs, 15m (49ft) in front and behind the goalkeeper.

A1 passes to A2, who tries to shoot. A1 becomes a defender and tries to stop him.

The ball now goes across to the B players who follow the same pattern. B2 tries to score.

Next, take turns as shown and play until everyone has had ten shots. The best score out of ten wins.

APPROACHES TO GOAL

To improve their chances of scoring, attackers need different strategies to outwit the goalkeeper and defenders. These are some you can use, on your own or working with teammates, to create good shooting opportunities as you reach the attacking third of the field.

CROSSING THE BALL

As a general rule you should try to pass the ball forward. Sometimes, however, it can be effective to pass the ball across, when you are on the wing in the attacking third – you can pass it to a teammate so that he can shoot. This is called crossing the ball.

This player is in a good position to try a header.

By using a long, high cross, this player sends the ball across the goalmouth.

Use a variety of passes to get the ball into the penalty area, so that a teammate can shoot as it crosses in front of the goal.

Once you have decided to cross the ball, cross it as soon as possible before defenders can take up good positions.

Make sure there is a teammate to make use of your cross. There is no point in crossing the ball straight to a defender or the goalkeeper.

SHOOTING FROM CROSSES

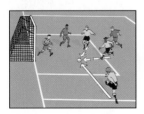

Check the position of other teammates. If you both try for the same cross a good chance may be lost.

If a defender is marking you, try to lose him just as your teammate crosses the ball.

Act really quickly when you see the opportunity to score and don't be intimidated by your opponents. Run for the ball and take a shot. Try to shoot down with a diving or downward header, or a volley.

DRAWING THE GOALKEEPER OUT

Goalkeepers often come out of goal as you approach, because this narrows down the area you can shoot at.

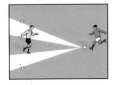

Here, it is difficult for the goalkeeper to cover the big areas that you can shoot at.

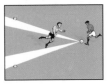

As he moves out the areas get smaller, but there is now a big space behind him.

If you can, use this opportunity to pass to a teammate out to the side so that he can shoot.

Even if the goalkeeper jumps at the right time, he will not be able to reach this high chip over his head.

You could also try chipping the ball, lifting it over the goalkeeper's head as he approaches and down into the goal. Make sure you send the ball high enough.

TURN AND SHOOT

There are often times when your back is to the goal. By turning to shoot quickly, you may take defenders by surprise. This exercise helps you practice this. It is for four players – a goalkeeper, a defender and two attackers.

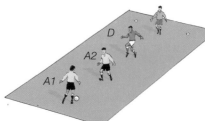

Mark out a goal. One attacker (A1) faces the goal. The other (A2) has his back to the goal and the defender (D) stands behind him.

You could use a wall pass.

A1 passes to A2, who has to turn quickly. A1 is now a supporting player, so A2 can pass to him or shoot. D tries to keep him from scoring.

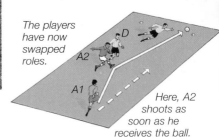

The players have now swapped roles.

Here, A2 shoots as soon as he receives the ball.

Take turns being the attackers. You could play as two teams of two and see which side does best as the attacking team.

ATTACKING PLAY

When your team has the ball, you are in attack, whatever your position. To play a good attacking game, you combine all the skills you have learned with a positive attitude and the determination to win. These two pages should help you develop the competitive edge that you need to do this.

FOUR PASS DRILL

To play this game, you need to use quick and varied passing skills. You need a big group – fourteen is best, but you could play with a few less or a few more. Mark out a field 50m (164ft) long and 30m (98ft) wide. Divide it into three equal areas.

30m (98ft)

'A' zone

50m (164ft)

'D' zone

'A' zone

1. Get into two groups of five attackers (A) and one group of four defenders (D). The Ds go into the middle zone, the As into the end zones. One A group has the ball.

2. These As pass the ball to each other four times while two of the defenders try to stop them. If the As succeed, they pass the ball over the D area to the other A team.

3. The other two defenders go into the other A area as the As try for four passes. If a D intercepts the ball at any time, he takes the place of the A who passed.

PASSING REMINDER TIPS

★ Communicate with your teammates so that they know where to pass.

★ If you don't have the ball, support by running around to find space.

★ Choose passes that you know you can carry out accurately.

★ Make use of give and go passes and crossover plays to avoid defenders.

★ Hold your pass until a teammate is in a position to receive it.

★ Unless you want to go over defenders, keep your passes as low as possible.

SMALL FIELD SHOOTING GAME

The area that you have for this game is very confined, so you have to make quick decisions and try to shoot as much as possible.

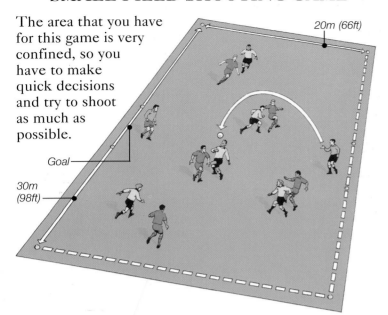

20m (66ft)

Goal

30m (98ft)

Mark out a field 20m (66ft) long and 30m (98ft) wide, and mark out two goals. You need at least ten players, in even numbers if possible.

Divide into two teams with a goalkeeper each. One goalkeeper starts the game each time by kicking the ball into the middle.

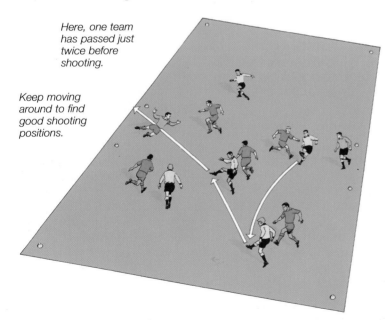

Here, one team has passed just twice before shooting.

Keep moving around to find good shooting positions.

Players from each team mark each other closely. Each team is only allowed up to three passes before trying a shot at goal.

If no one tries a shot after three consecutive passes, the ball goes over to the other team. Keep a record of the score.

STAR SHOT

Being an attacker or striker takes lots of determination and courage. If you watch star players, you will see that they do not hesitate to take opportunities to go for the ball and shoot.

This is Brazilian attacker Juninho playing at full stretch in a match against Sweden.

SHOOTING REMINDER TIPS

★ Always take a shot if you see an opportunity. Don't worry that you might miss.

★ Vary your shots. Try shots from difficult angles, not just in front of the goal.

★ Keep alert when your team shoots. There may be a rebound opportunity.

★ Use crosses to make opportunities for diving headers and volleys.

★ Keep the ball down and aim for the bottom corners of the goal.

★ Make your shots accurate rather than powerful.

WORLD SOCCER QUIZ

16. Which of these national teams plays in orange shirts and white shorts?

a. Denmark
b. Holland
c. Germany

17. What is the claim to fame of the Centenario Stadium in Montevideo?

a. It is the world's largest
b. It was the first to have an artificial surface
c. It was the first to stage a World Cup game

18. Who captained England's World Cup winning squad of 1966?

a. Geoff Hurst
b. Bobby Moore
c. Bryan Robson

19. In 1994, Russia's Oleg Salenko set an individual record for goals scored in a World Cup game. How many times did he score?

a. 4
b. 5
c. 6

20. What was special about the World Cup game between Yugoslavia and France on June 16, 1954?

a. It was the first televised World Cup game
b. The scoreline was the highest ever
c. It was the first time substitutes were allowed

21. Which country hosted the 1995 Women's World Cup?

a. Sweden
b. Germany
c. Argentina

22. Which international team played in its first World Cup in 1994?

a. Nigeria
b. Chile
c. Egypt

23. In 1994, Cameroon striker Roger Milla became the oldest man to score in a World Cup game. How old was he?

a. 38
b. 41
c. 45

24. Which country won the 1995 Under 17 World Championship?

a. Ghana
b. Italy
c. Romania

25. What is the emblem on England's team uniform?

a. A unicorn
b. Three lions
c. A red cross

26. Which player was voted FIFA World Footballer of the Year in 1995?

a. Gianluca Vialli
b. Paolo Maldini
c. George Weah

27. What was Khalid Ismail Mubarak given as a reward for scoring the United Arab Emirates' first ever World Cup goal?

a. A Rolls Royce
b. A gold-plated soccer ball
c. $100,000

28. Which international team has played in the most World Cup Finals?

a. Italy
b. Brazil
c. West Germany

29. Until 1991, the leading goal scorer in Europe each year was given a special award. What was it called?

a. The EuroStriker Bowl
b. The UEFA Medal
c. The Golden Boot

30. Who of the following has not been a manager of the England national team?

a. Glen Hoddle
b. Graham Taylor
c. Bryan Robson

31. What does Chilean player Carlos Caszely hold the unfortunate record for being?

a. The first player to be given a red card in a World Cup game
b. The first player to score a World Cup own goal
c. The player who has missed the most World Cup penalties

SOCCER QUIZ
?

PART THREE
DEAD BALL SKILLS

CONTENTS

DEAD BALL BASICS

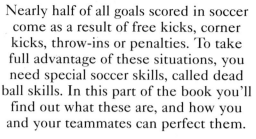

Nearly half of all goals scored in soccer come as a result of free kicks, corner kicks, throw-ins or penalties. To take full advantage of these situations, you need special soccer skills, called dead ball skills. In this part of the book you'll find out what these are, and how you and your teammates can perfect them.

This player is getting ready to take a penalty (see page 28).

WHAT IS A DEAD BALL?

Every so often in a soccer game, a player will hit the ball off the field, break one of the rules, score a goal, or suffer an injury. In each case the game stops temporarily. The ball is said to be 'out of play', or 'dead'. To restart the game, you have to use a particular kind of kick or throw to bring the dead ball back into play.

Because a dead ball is out of play, you can use your hands to place it before you take the restart kick.

RESTART KICKS AND THROWS

If the ball goes off the field, play is restarted with a goal kick, corner kick or throw-in, depending on where the ball left the field.

If the game stops because a player has broken a soccer rule, it is restarted with a free kick or, in certain cases, a penalty kick.

Whenever a player scores a goal, or after a break in play between periods of the game, the game is restarted with a center kick.

If play is stopped for any other reason, such as injury, it is restarted with a drop ball. You'll find out more about each type of restart later on.

DEAD BALL ADVANTAGES

Here, the team in red is about to take a free kick. This typical dead ball situation shows three of the main advantages of playing the ball when it is dead, rather than when it is in normal, 'open' play.

★ You have plenty of time and space. The other team's players have to stand a set distance away, and cannot interfere by tackling or obstructing you.

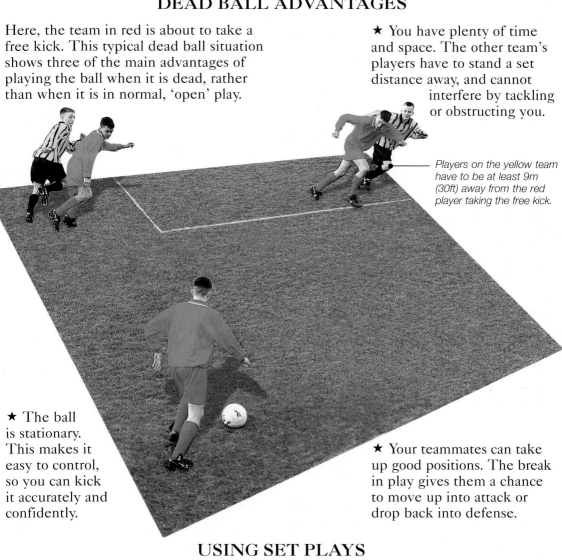

Players on the yellow team have to be at least 9m (30ft) away from the red player taking the free kick.

★ The ball is stationary. This makes it easy to control, so you can kick it accurately and confidently.

★ Your teammates can take up good positions. The break in play gives them a chance to move up into attack or drop back into defense.

USING SET PLAYS

The other major advantage of a dead ball is that it gives you a chance to use a carefully pre-planned team move, or 'set play'. You can rehearse various set plays in practice, and use them to outwit your opponents during a game.

Throughout this part of the book you'll find field diagrams. These show specific set plays for you and your teammates to try. On these diagrams, a dotted red arrow shows the path of a player and a solid blue arrow shows the path of the ball.

This set play diagram shows the free kick move that the red players are about to use in the picture above.

This player has drawn his opponent away to make space for his teammate to receive the ball.

SOCCER WORDS

To explain the techniques and tactics involved in playing a dead ball, this part of the book uses a number of soccer words. These pages give you a reminder of the basic soccer terms, and introduce a few new ones that you'll come across as you read about dead ball skills.

FINDING YOUR WAY AROUND THE FIELD

If you kick the ball toward your opponents' goal, you are playing it **upfield**. Toward you own goal is **downfield**.

The **wings** are the edges of the field along either sideline. A ball played across from either wing to the middle of the field is a **cross**.

The third of the field nearest to your own goal is your team's **defending third**.

The middle third of the field is the **midfield**.

The third of the field nearest your opponents' goal is your team's **attacking third**.

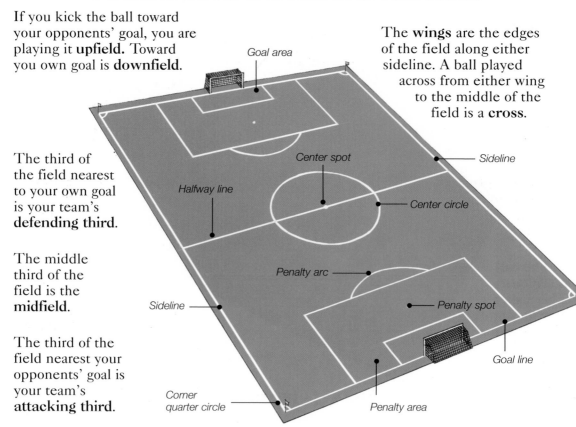

Goal area

Center spot

Halfway line

Sideline

Center circle

Penalty arc

Sideline

Penalty spot

Corner quarter circle

Penalty area

Goal line

THE REFEREE

The **referee** is an official who controls a soccer game. It is his job to decide when to stop and restart play. He uses a whistle and special arm signals (which you will read about later) to show the players his decisions.

LINESMEN

Two **linesmen** help the referee by watching the game from opposite sides of the field. Each linesman uses a flag to signal to the referee if the ball goes out of play or if he sees a player breaking any of the soccer rules.

TYPES OF PLAYERS

A soccer team is made up of a **goalkeeper,** or "goalie", who guards his team's goal, and ten **outfield** players. Each outfield player **marks** a member of the other team. This means keeping close to him to stop him from receiving or moving with the ball.

This player is marking his opponent closely.

This defender is clearing the ball from his penalty area.

This midfield player has won the ball and is about to pass.

This forward has found space to try a shot at goal.

Defenders play mostly in their defending third. Their main job is to prevent the other team's players from having a chance to score.

Midfield players are the link between defense and attack. They move the ball upfield, and try to pass to a teammate who can score.

Forwards push upfield into the attacking third, hoping to receive a pass which will give them a chance to shoot at goal.

WHAT DOES OFFSIDES MEAN?

You are not allowed to play the ball while you are in an **offsides** position. You are offsides if you are nearer to your opponents' goal line than the ball at the moment it is passed to you, unless there are two or more opposing players at least as close to their goal line. You can't be offsides if you are within your own half of the field.

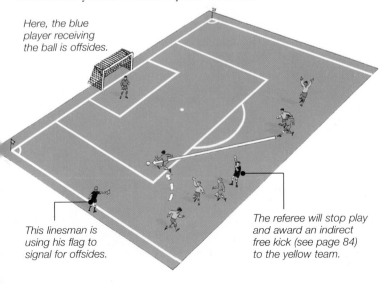

Here, the blue player receiving the ball is offsides.

This linesman is using his flag to signal for offsides.

The referee will stop play and award an indirect free kick (see page 84) to the yellow team.

FOOT PARTS

Most dead ball skills involve using one of these three different parts of your foot.

The **instep,** or **inside** of your foot, is the part from your big toe to your ankle.

The **outside** of your foot is the part from your little toe back to your ankle.

The **top,** or **laces** is the area on the upper part of your foot, covered by your shoelaces.

CENTER KICKS

The referee tosses a coin to decide which team kicks off.

Every soccer game begins with a center kick. This first dead ball opportunity, called the 'kick-off', gives you an early chance to take control. Center kicks are also used to get the second half underway, to restart the game whenever a team scores a goal, and to begin any periods of extra time.

Wait for the referee to blow his whistle before you take the kick.

CENTER KICK RULES

All center kicks are taken from the center spot. When you take the kick, every player must be in his own half. Once you've kicked the ball, you mustn't kick it again until it has been touched by another player. You can't score straight from the center spot.

Opposing players must be outside the center circle when you take the kick.

You have to play the ball forward from the spot, into the other team's half.

A SHORT, SAFE CENTER KICK

A center kick gives you possession of the ball in midfield. To keep possession, so that you can control play, use a short pass to a teammate standing alongside you in the center circle.

Use your instep to tap the ball forward gently into the path of your teammate.

Make sure the ball crosses the halfway line completely.

Your teammate can quickly pass the ball to one of your team's players who has space to receive it without being challenged.

PRESSURING YOUR OPPONENTS

STAR CENTER

You can use a longer center kick to move play upfield quickly and put pressure on the other team.

Kick the ball upfield into the attacking third. Aim for a space behind the other team's midfield players.

Your forwards should sprint upfield from the halfway line to challenge for possession.

This tactic might well cause your team to lose the ball, but it can sometimes create an early scoring chance.

Here, the Croatian players Alen Boksic and Davor Suker talk tactics as they prepare to take a center kick. Unless their team is trailing in the late stages of a game, they will probably opt for a short center kick to make sure that their team keeps possession of the ball.

CREATING AN OVERLOAD

If you decide to try a long center kick, your team will have a better chance of winning the ball if several of your players gather on one side of the field.

Angle your kick to the 'overloaded' side of the field, into the path of your forwards.

The other team may realize what you are planning, and move across to the overloaded side of the field.

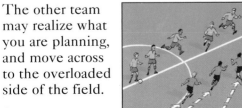

In this case, try switching your center kick move at the last minute, playing the ball to the other side.

THROW-IN TECHNIQUE

A linesman points his flag like this to signal a throw-in.

If an opposing player knocks the ball over either sideline, one of your team's players has to throw it back onto the field. This is known as taking a throw-in. It is the only type of restart which involves using your hands to bring a dead ball back into play.

The team playing in the direction of the flag takes the throw.

THROW-IN RULES

To throw the ball back into play you have to bring it forward from behind your head, using both hands. As you release the ball, part of both your feet must be touching the ground, on or behind the sideline.

You cannot score a goal by throwing the ball straight into your opponents' goal.

Feet on ground, on or behind sideline.

HOW TO HOLD THE BALL

Make sure that you hold the ball with your fingers spread around its back and sides. Your thumbs should nearly touch.

Holding the ball like this lets you control it more easily as you release your throw.

PRACTICING YOUR THROW-IN

You need to be able to throw accurately or you may give away the ball. To improve your throw, try this exercise with a partner.

Stand about 10m (33ft) apart. Use throw-ins to pass the ball back and forth. Throw the ball to your partner's feet so that he can control it easily.

As you get better at throwing the ball, your partner can give you a specific target area. Try throwing to your partner's head, chest and thigh.

TAKING A LONGER THROW-IN

Most professional soccer teams have at least one player who specializes in throwing the ball a long way. Practice the technique shown here to develop a long, accurate throw-in.

Arch your back to bring the ball as far back as possible.

Place your leading foot close behind the sideline.

At least part of your trailing foot must be touching the ground.

Use your hands and fingers to direct the ball's flight.

Leading leg

Hold the ball in front of your head and take a couple of quick steps toward the sideline.

Take a long final stride to reach the line, bringing the ball back behind your head.

With the weight on your leading leg, whip the upper part of your body forward to catapult the ball away.

THROWING AWAY POSSESSION

If you break one of the rules when you take a throw-in, the referee will ask the other team to retake the throw. Be careful not to lose possession with a foul throw. The pictures below show the things you need to avoid to keep your throw-in legal.

FOUL THROW - The player's feet are too far over the sideline for a legal throw-in.

FOUL THROW - The thrower's right foot is off the ground as he releases the ball.

FOUL THROW - The player hasn't brought the ball far enough back over his head.

STAR THROW

Here, Gary Neville, playing for Manchester United, prepares to launch a long throw-in along the wing.

THROW-IN TACTICS

A throw-in is more than just a way of bringing the ball back onto the field. A good throw can start an attacking move, or ease the pressure on your defense. You and your teammates can use the tactics introduced here to make the most of throw-in moves during a game.

THROW-IN TIPS

Always try to throw to a teammate who can receive the ball without being challenged. Whenever possible, and especially in your own half, send the ball upfield.

Several of your players should move into throwing range to increase your choice of receiver.

As you prepare to throw, your teammates need to find open space by moving away from marking players.

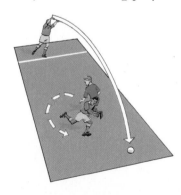

A throw into an open space, for a teammate to run onto, is often more effective than one aimed directly at him.

You can even throw over a teammate into open space behind him, so that he can turn and chase the ball.

You can often catch the other team off guard if the member of your team nearest to the ball when it goes out of play takes the throw-in quickly. However quickly you throw, make sure you bring the ball back over your head.

A DECOY MOVE

As you prepare to throw, your teammates can use a decoy move like this to create space for a particular player to receive the ball.

1. Player A starts an angled run as though to receive the throw, drawing his marking player away with him.

2. Player B, running in from the opposite angle, moves into the space created by Player A's 'decoy run'.

3. The thrower delivers his throw into the path of player B, who can receive the ball unchallenged and push upfield into attack.

USING A WALL PASS THROW-IN

Once you've taken a throw, get right back into play. By using one of your team-mates as a 'wall' to knock your throw back to you, you can rejoin the action immediately. This wall pass move is particularly useful if all your players are closely marked.

1. Throw to a nearby team-mate's feet, so that he can control the ball easily.

Move forward onto the field.

2. The receiver uses his instep to hit a first touch pass back to you.

3. You can build on this basic wall pass move by playing the ball upfield for the player who first received your throw to run onto.

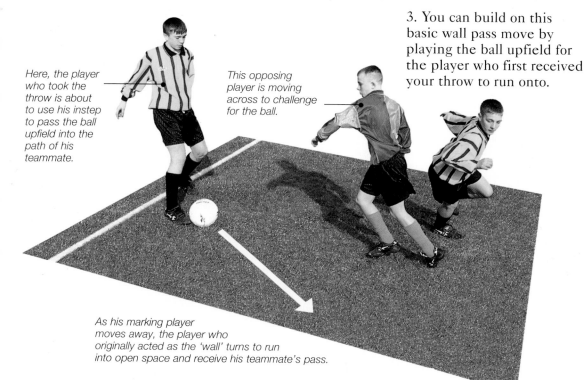

Here, the player who took the throw is about to use his instep to pass the ball upfield into the path of his teammate.

This opposing player is moving across to challenge for the ball.

As his marking player moves away, the player who originally acted as the 'wall' turns to run into open space and receive his teammate's pass.

THROWING INTO THE PENALTY AREA

If your team is awarded a throw-in within the attacking third, try using a long throw into the penalty area. Your teammates can't be offside from a throw-in, so they can move upfield to threaten your opponents' goal.

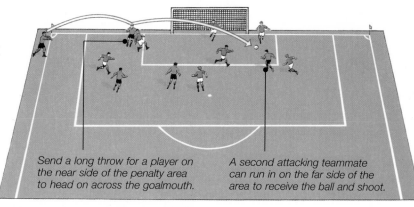

Send a long throw for a player on the near side of the penalty area to head on across the goalmouth.

A second attacking teammate can run in on the far side of the area to receive the ball and shoot.

GOAL KICKS

If a player on the other team knocks the ball out of play over your goal line, a member of your team has to restart the game with a goal kick. Like center kicks, goal kicks give you a chance either to control possession of the ball or move play upfield quickly.

The referee will point at the goal area to signal a goal kick.

GOAL KICK RULES

To bring the ball back into play with a goal kick, you have to kick it from within your goal area, so that it leaves the penalty area. You can't kick the ball again until another player has touched it.

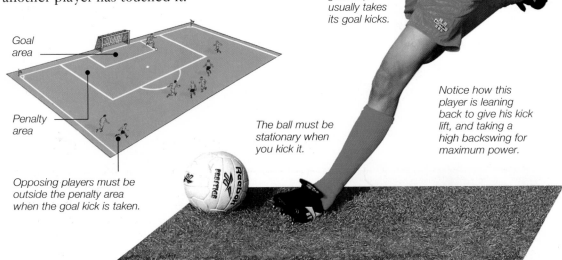

Goal area

Penalty area

Opposing players must be outside the penalty area when the goal kick is taken.

A team's goalkeeper usually takes its goal kicks.

The ball must be stationary when you kick it.

Notice how this player is leaning back to give his kick lift, and taking a high backswing for maximum power.

THE OUTFIELD KICKER OPTION

If your goalkeeper makes a bad goal kick, an opposing player may intercept the ball and shoot while your goalie is out of position. You may prefer one of your outfield players to take the kick, so that your goalkeeper can stay in position.

There is a drawback to an outfield player taking a goal kick. It makes it harder for your defenders to catch opposing players offsides (see page 69) after the kick. The kicker should rush forward to get level with his teammates as quickly as he can.

TAKING A LONG GOAL KICK

You can use a long goal kick to move play out of your team's defensive third. Use the kicking technique shown here to send the ball as far upfield as you can. By hitting the ball below its midline, you can make it rise and travel over players.

Lift your kicking foot in a high backswing.

Lean back slightly as you kick.

Use your arms for balance.

Take a short run up, from a slight angle, so that you can strike the ball with force.

With a long last stride, get your nonkicking foot slightly behind and to the side of the ball.

Swing your kicking foot forward to strike the lower half of the ball with your laces.

Follow through with your kicking leg to power the ball as far upfield as possible.

AIMING

Try to pick out a teammate with your long goal kick, or at least aim it where there are enough of your players to stand a good chance of winning the ball. Here Dino Baggio (Italy) and John Sheridan (Republic of Ireland) challenge for a long goal kick ball.

USING A SHORTER GOAL KICK

You can make sure that your team keeps possession of the ball by sending a shorter goal kick to an unmarked teammate near your own penalty area. Be careful to deliver the ball so that it is easy to control. Some of your midfield players can drop back into your defending third so that at least one of your teammates is free to receive the ball safely.

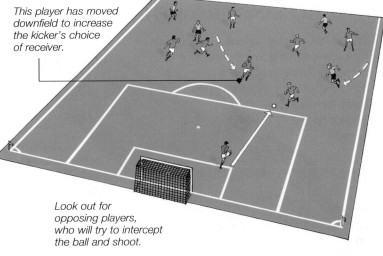

This player has moved downfield to increase the kicker's choice of receiver.

Look out for opposing players, who will try to intercept the ball and shoot.

CORNER KICKS

When a defending player hits the ball over his own goal line, the referee awards the attacking team a corner kick. This gives you a chance to play the ball across your opponents' goalmouth for a teammate to shoot at goal.

To signal a corner, the referee points to the corner flag.

You have to take a corner kick with the corner flag in position.

CORNER KICK RULES

To take a corner, you kick the ball from within the corner quarter circle nearest to the point where it went out of play.

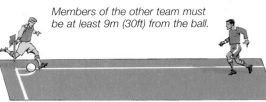

Members of the other team must be at least 9m (30ft) from the ball.

You're not allowed to play the ball again until another player has touched it.

PLACING THE BALL FOR A CORNER KICK

You need to place the ball in the corner circle in such a way that you can kick it without the flag blocking your run up or swing. The best place to put the ball will depend on whether you are left- or right-footed.

Here, the ball is placed correctly for a left-footed corner kicker.

Here, the ball is placed correctly for a right-footed corner kicker.

CROSSING FROM THE CORNER

If you hit a long, lofted corner kick to a teammate just beyond the far side of the goal, he'll have a chance to shoot from behind the goalkeeper's view.

A player who receives a corner kick can't be offsides, so your teammates can move up toward the goalmouth to receive your corner cross.

INSWINGERS

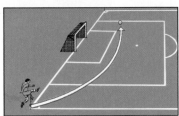

You can make your cross even more effective by bending it, so that the ball swings in toward the goal. A corner kick like this is known as an inswinger.

HOW DO YOU BEND A CORNER KICK?

The secret to bending a corner kick cross is to strike the ball off-center so that it spins as it travels through the air. The easiest way to do this is to use the instep of your kicking foot to strike the outside edge of the ball. This right-footed player is about to hit an inswinger from the left corner in this way.

You also need to remember to hit the ball below its midline, so that your cross has plenty of lift.

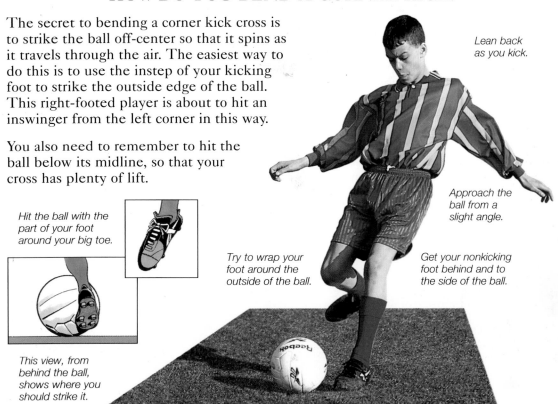

Lean back as you kick.

Approach the ball from a slight angle.

Hit the ball with the part of your foot around your big toe.

Try to wrap your foot around the outside of the ball.

Get your nonkicking foot behind and to the side of the ball.

This view, from behind the ball, shows where you should strike it.

PRACTICING YOUR CROSS

As you get better at judging the distance, see how much you can bend each cross.

Practice this with a partner to get used to the length and height of a good cross. Stand on the front corners of the penalty area – or about 40m (130ft) apart if you're not on a field. This is about the distance from the corner to the farthest post. Hit crosses to one another, trying to deliver the ball so that your partner can catch it just above his head.

WHO KICKS?

Bending a kick using your instep makes the ball swing away to the left if you're right-footed, or to the right if you're left-footed. Make sure that you pick the correct player to take an inswinger from a particular side of the field.

A right-footed player takes inswingers from left of the goal.

A left-footed player takes inswingers from right of the goal.

CORNER KICK MOVES

A cross from the corner is an example of a 'fifty-fifty' ball, as both teams have an equal chance of gaining possession. You can tip the balance in your team's favor by using a preplanned corner move. These pages suggest several corner kick set plays for you to try.

FINDING SPACE TO RECEIVE A CROSS

For any corner kick move to be successful, one of your teammates in the penalty area needs to be free to receive the ball and shoot. As you prepare to take a corner, your forwards should try to move away from their marking players to find space.

Here, the blue forwards are getting ready to receive a cross from the right-hand corner.

The blue players in the far side of the penalty area can strike from a long cross or a flicked-on ball (see below).

This blue player is trying to find space to receive a shorter, driven cross (see page 82).

There is a good chance for a shot into this side of the goal, which the red team has left unguarded.

A FLICK-ON FROM THE NEAR POST

For this move, one of your teammates needs to move into space around the goal-post nearest to the corner that you are kicking from. Send a short, inswinging cross to this player at the near post.

The player receiving the corner cross uses his head to flick the ball on across goal. One of your other forwards runs in on the far side of the goal area to receive the flicked-on ball and shoot.

Judge your cross so that your teammate can head the ball.

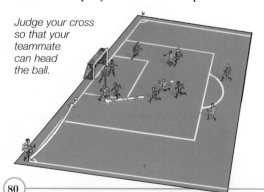

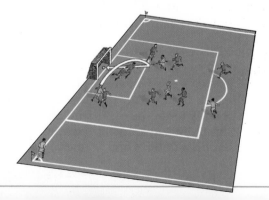

LAYING THE BALL BACK

This alternative near post move can be as effective as a flick-on across the goal. Send a cross to a teammate at the near post. Instead of heading the ball across the goalmouth, the receiver 'lays it back'.
This means heading it down into the path of a teammate running in from midfield.

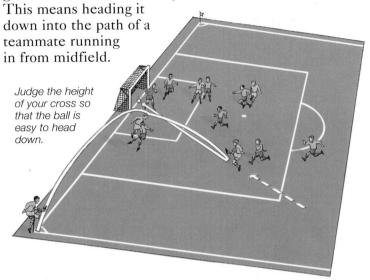

Judge the height of your cross so that the ball is easy to head down.

CORNER ACTION

Try to spot different corner moves when you watch professional players in action. Here, the left-footed corner taker has hit an inswinging corner cross. His teammates in the goal area will try to head the ball down into the goal.

OUTSWINGING CORNERS

Another option is to bend your corner kick cross away from the goalmouth. This kind of corner is called an 'outswinger'. It makes it easier for your teammates moving toward goal to head the ball well.

Players can run onto your cross from the edge of the penalty area.

Play your cross so that the ball swings out toward the penalty spot.

By moving out toward the corner, or over toward the far post, your teammates can draw defenders away from the near side of the penalty area. This creates space for a player to run onto a shorter outswinging cross.

This player is drawing away his marking player to create space.

WHO KICKS?

As with inswingers (see page 79), you need to pick the correct kicker to take an outswinging corner from a particular side of the field.

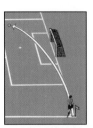

A right-footed player takes outswinging corners from the right-hand side of the goal.

A left-footed player takes outswinging corners from the left-hand side of the goal.

SHORT AND DRIVEN CORNERS

Because a swinging cross is the most popular corner kick option, it is also the most predictable. To keep the other team guessing, vary your corner kick tactics every now and then. You can use a driven corner for a faster-paced cross, or a short corner for an attack from a different angle.

TAKING A DRIVEN CORNER

When you hit a swinging, lofted cross, the ball takes a long time to reach the goal area because it follows a curved path through the air. By striking a low, straight, powerful cross, you can send the ball across the goalmouth more quickly.

As you run up, get your nonkicking foot up alongside the ball. Don't lean back. Keep your body upright and over the ball.

With your knee over the ball, and your toes pointing down, strike the ball just below its center with the top of your foot.

Follow through with your kicking leg to power the ball across into the penalty area. It will travel in a straight line, rising slightly.

DRIVEN CORNER MOVES

Try to send a driven corner either to a player on the near side of the goal area, or one around the middle of the penalty area. A driven cross will stay low, so the receiver must be prepared to kick a waist-high volley, or even try a diving header. Your other teammates can create space for him by moving as though to receive a longer cross (see page 78) or a short corner (see page 83).

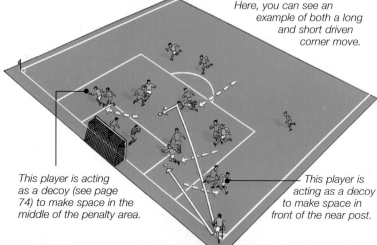

Here, you can see an example of both a long and short driven corner move.

This player is acting as a decoy (see page 74) to make space in the middle of the penalty area.

This player is acting as a decoy to make space in front of the near post.

PLAYING A SHORT CORNER

You can use this simple pass and return tactic, or 'short corner', to build up an attacking move from the corner of the field.

One of your teammates moves within easy passing range of the corner. Send the ball along the ground to this nearby player.

As soon as you have taken the kick, run into open space downfield from your teammate, so that he can pass the ball back to you.

Use your instep to pass the ball to your teammate.

Run on to collect the return pass.

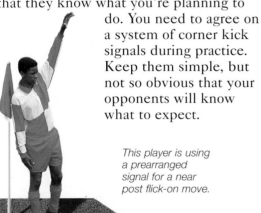

A move like this lets you dribble the ball toward goal to hit a cross from closer in, or try a shot yourself.

SIGNALING THE MOVE

When you've decided what kind of corner move to use, signal to your teammates so that they know what you're planning to do. You need to agree on a system of corner kick signals during practice. Keep them simple, but not so obvious that your opponents will know what to expect.

This player is using a prearranged signal for a near post flick-on move.

CORNER SKILLS GAME

Mark out a special field, 40m (130ft) wide but only about 15m (49ft) long. Play a game of five- or seven-a-side within this area. The short, wide field means that most of the action takes place around either goalmouth. This gives you lots of chances to try out different corner moves.

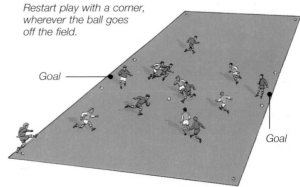

Restart play with a corner, wherever the ball goes off the field.

Goal

Goal

FREE KICK BASICS

The referee puts his arm out to signal a direct free kick.

If one of your opponents 'commits an offense' by breaking a soccer rule, the referee will stop the game and ask your team to restart play with a free kick. There are two types of free kicks – direct, to punish serious offenses, and indirect for less serious ones.

To signal an indirect free kick, the referee raises his arm.

SERIOUS OFFENSES

The referee will award a direct free kick if a player kicks, trips, charges, strikes, pushes, holds or jumps at an opponent; if an outfield player deliberately uses his hands to control the ball, or if a goalkeeper handles the ball outside his penalty area.

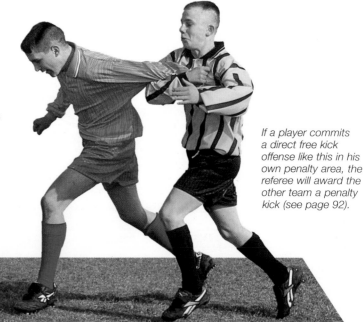

Here, the player in yellow is holding his opponent back, rather than playing the ball. An unfair challenge like this is known as a foul.

If a player commits a direct free kick offense like this in his own penalty area, the referee will award the other team a penalty kick (see page 92).

INDIRECT FREE KICK OFFENSES

These pictures show the offenses for which a referee will award an indirect free kick. The three types of offenses illustrated on the top row are specifically for goalkeepers.

Time-wasting by holding the ball for a long time.

Using hands to receive a backpass from a teammate.

Taking more than four steps while holding the ball.

Charging or obstructing the opposing goalkeeper.

Playing dangerously (here, kicking a high ball).

Charging or obstructing a player who isn't on the ball.

Receiving the ball while in an offsides position (see page 5).

FREE KICK RULES

To take a free kick, you kick the ball from the point on the field where the offense took place. The ball must be stationary when you kick it, and the other team's players have to be at least 9m (30ft) away. You can't play the ball again until it has been touched by another player.

If the free kick is direct, you are allowed to score straight from the kick.

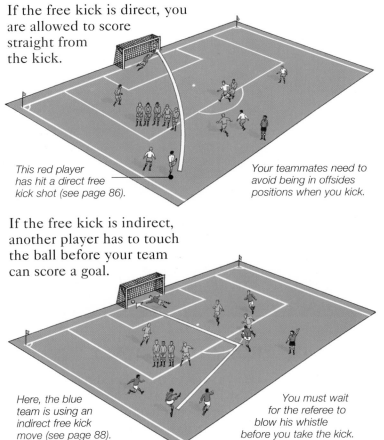

This red player has hit a direct free kick shot (see page 86).

Your teammates need to avoid being in offsides positions when you kick.

If the free kick is indirect, another player has to touch the ball before your team can score a goal.

Here, the blue team is using an indirect free kick move (see page 88).

You must wait for the referee to blow his whistle before you take the kick.

SPECIAL CASES

If you are awarded a free kick in your own penalty area, you have to kick the ball out of the penalty area to bring it back into play.

Opposing players must be outside the penalty area when you kick.

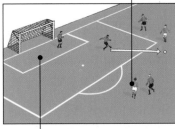

If the kick is inside your goal area, you can take it from any part of that area.

If you are given an indirect free kick inside your opponent's goal area, you take the kick from the edge of the goal area.

Your opponents are allowed to stand on their goal line, between the posts, despite being less than 9m (30ft) away.

TAKING A FREE KICK IN YOUR OWN HALF

The top priority when you take a free kick in your own half of the field is to make sure that your team keeps the ball. Use a simple pass to a player in open space.

Aim your kick away from any nearby opponent hoping to steal the ball.

Send the ball upfield whenever possible.

DIRECT FREE KICKS

A free kick in the attacking third gives you a good chance to score a spectacular goal. You're most likely to score if you keep your free kick move simple. These pages look at the simplest of all attacking free kicks – a direct shot at goal from the edge of the penalty area.

THE DEFENSIVE WALL

When you take a free kick near the penalty area, your opponents will usually protect their goalmouth by forming a defensive wall. Several players will stand side by side to block your shooting line. To score, you need to get the ball past this wall of players.

The players in the wall will try to block one side of the goalmouth, while their goalkeeper guards the other.

BENDING YOUR SHOT AROUND THE WALL

By striking the outside edge of the ball with your instep, you can bend a free kick so that it swings away to your nonkicking side. Don't hit the ball too low down or it will rise over the goal.

To bend a kick in the other direction, so that it swings out to your kicking side, use the outside of your foot to strike the inside edge of the ball. Keep the toes of your kicking foot pointed down as you kick.

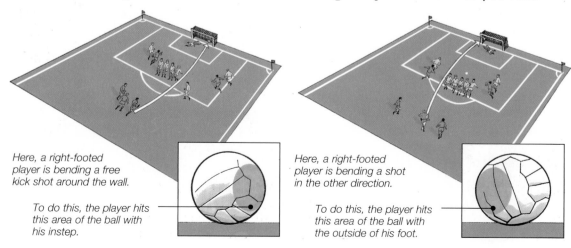

Here, a right-footed player is bending a free kick shot around the wall.

To do this, the player hits this area of the ball with his instep.

Here, a right-footed player is bending a shot in the other direction.

To do this, the player hits this area of the ball with the outside of his foot.

BENDING SHOT PRACTICE

To practice your swerving shot, put one corner flag in the center of the goal, and another on the penalty spot. Place the ball on the penalty arc, in line with the flags. Try to bend a kick around one side of the nearest flag into the other side of the goalmouth.

Try bending shots in either direction.

Try placing the ball farther around the arc so that you have to bend your kick more.

SHOOTING STAR

Here, Roberto Baggio is powering a bending free kick shot at goal. One of his Juventus teammates helps to shield the move until the last moment.

USING A FAKE CROSSOVER

You can use this tactic to disguise the direction of a direct free kick shot.

1. You and a teammate (ideally a player who kicks with the opposite foot to you) both prepare as though to take the kick.

2. Your teammate runs up to the ball, as though to shoot, but steps over it at the last minute.

Your teammate's run will help to hide your shot.

3. Time your own run up so that just after your teammate fakes a shot, you hit a powerful shot at goal. Your teammate can continue his run to follow in your shot.

FREE KICK MOVES

Even if you can hit a hard, swerving shot, you are unlikely to score from a free kick unless you can create an element of surprise. You need to leave your opponents unsure which direction your attack will come from. Use one of the moves described here to baffle the defense.

STRETCHING THE WALL

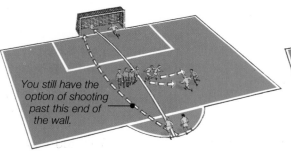

You still have the option of shooting past this end of the wall.

One or two of your teammates join the end of the defensive wall, to block the goalkeeper's view of the free kick.

As you take the kick, your players in the wall break away to let your shot past, turning to follow it in.

MAKING YOUR OWN WALL

Two or three of your teammates form a separate wall a few feet in front of the ball to hide the kick from view.

Your players move off as you kick. They need to hide the ball as long as possible, without getting in its way.

CREATING A GAP IN THE WALL

This move requires split-second timing. One or two of your forwards try to squeeze right up in front of the middle of the defensive wall. By moving away from the wall as you shoot, they may be able to create a gap for your shot to pass through.

Your players musn't move off too soon or the wall will close up.

INDIRECT MOVES

From an indirect free kick you have to pass the ball before a player can shoot. A simple pass to one side lets you quickly change the angle of your attack so that one of your teammates can have a clear shot at goal.

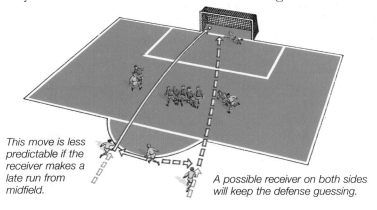

This move is less predictable if the receiver makes a late run from midfield.

A possible receiver on both sides will keep the defense guessing.

THE BACK PASS SWITCH

You can try this move to switch the direction of an indirect free kick attack. Approach the ball as though to kick to a teammate on one side. Instead, roll the ball backward to a player on the other side to shoot.

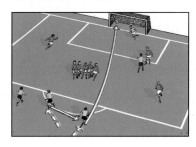

Use the underside of your foot to roll the ball to a teammate behind you.

TWO-PASS MOVES

Using two passes in a free kick move lets you move the ball to one side of the wall and closer to the goal, for a good shooting position. Try this basic two-pass move.

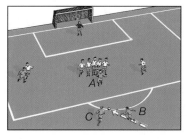

Player A takes up a position slightly downfield from the wall, facing back toward the ball. Left-footed player B and right-footed player C both prepare as though to take the free kick.

Player B does a fake over the ball, running on diagonally to one side of the wall. As he does so, player C sends a pass along the ground to player A in front of the wall. He in turn passes the ball sideways for player B to run onto and shoot at goal.

MORE FREE KICK MOVES

You need to prepare suitable moves for free kicks from different positions in the attacking third. On these pages you can see some suggested moves for free kicks near either wing. You can also find out how you and your teammates can perfect your own free kick moves.

FREE KICKS FROM THE WING

When your team is awarded a free kick at either side of your opponent's penalty area, the other team's players will usually move out to be level with their defensive wall. This stops your teammates from taking up positions near the goal, where they would be offsides.

In a free kick situation like this, you can attack by crossing the ball into space behind the defense, for your teammates to run onto.

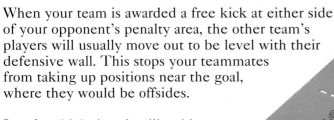

Here, the blue player taking the free kick has hit a long, outswinging cross from the wing.

Each forward times his run so as to avoid being offsides.

DISGUISING A FREE KICK CROSS

Try using this set play to disguise a free kick cross to the near post.

1. Player A, a left-footer, runs in as if to take the free kick. At the same time, players C and D move off as if to receive a long, outswinging cross to the far post.

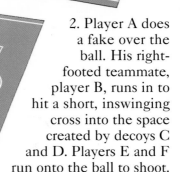

2. Player A does a fake over the ball. His right-footed teammate, player B, runs in to hit a short, inswinging cross into the space created by decoys C and D. Players E and F run onto the ball to shoot.

USING THE WING

A cross from a free kick at the side of the penalty area is fairly predictable. You may be able to surprise your opponents by using a move along the wing. Send the ball toward the sideline, into the path of a player making a run from midfield.

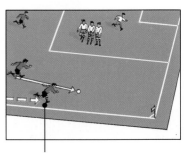

The receiver can dribble the ball upfield along the wing and send a cross into the goal area.

PRACTICING YOUR OWN FREE KICK MOVES

You can try out some of your own set plays for attacking free kicks by having a free kick competition. Split into two teams of seven or eight players. Each team takes one direct and one indirect free kick from each of five different positions outside the penalty area, while the other team defends the goal. The team which scores the most goals from their ten free kick attempts wins.

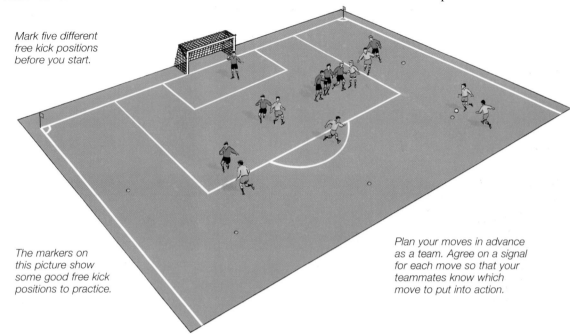

Mark five different free kick positions before you start.

The markers on this picture show some good free kick positions to practice.

Plan your moves in advance as a team. Agree on a signal for each move so that your teammates know which move to put into action.

★ Always take into consideration whether the kick is direct or indirect, and what position it is from.

★ Keep your free kick moves fairly simple. Ideally they should involve no more than three touches.

★ Remember that you cannot use any move that involves a teammate being in an offsides position.

VARYING YOUR CHOICE OF MOVE

Whichever attacking free kick move you use, it is unlikely to work if your opponents can tell what you're planning from the position of your players. Try to vary which move you use from each position. As an example, the pictures below show three very different moves involving a teammate positioned at one end of the defensive wall.

By breaking away from the wall, the forward has here distracted attention from his teammate's direct shot.

Here, the forward has moved out from the wall to take part in an indirect two-pass move (see page 89).

In this case, the player on the end of the wall has turned to run onto a ball chipped over the top of the wall.

PENALTIES

To signal a penalty, the referee points at the penalty spot.

When a player commits a serious offense inside his own penalty area, the referee awards the attacking team a penalty kick. A penalty is a high-pressure, 'one-on-one' situation in which you try to beat your opponents' goalkeeper with a direct shot at goal.

Place the ball yourself, so that you know it is on a sound surface.

PENALTY RULES

To take a penalty, you shoot at goal from the penalty spot. You can't play the ball again until it has been touched by another player.

The goalkeeper can't move until you play the ball.

All other players must be outside the penalty area, beyond the arc, and downfield from the spot.

STAYING COOL

When you take a penalty, don't be indecisive or hesitant. Pick your target area and concentrate on hitting a hard, low shot into that part of the goal.

A firmly hit shot just inside either post will be extremely hard to stop.

SHOOTING WITH POWER

1. The key to a low, hard shot is to keep your body over the ball as you kick, rather than leaning back.

2. Get your nonkicking foot alongside the ball so that the knee of your kicking leg is over the ball.

3. With your toes pointing down, use the top of your kicking foot to drive the ball forward.

Use your arms for balance.

Follow through with your kicking leg for maximum power.

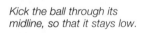

Kick the ball through its midline, so that it stays low.

SOFT OPTION

You may find it easier to place your penalty kick shot accurately by hitting the ball with slightly less power, using your instep.

FOLLOWING UP THE PENALTY

Your teammates should be ready to close in on the goalmouth as soon as you've taken your penalty kick.

If the goalkeeper blocks your shot, the ball may rebound to provide another chance.

THE PENALTY SHOOT-OUT

If the scores are tied at the end of overtime, the teams often have a penalty competition to decide which team wins the game. This is known as a penalty 'shoot-out'. If one team has scored more goals after both teams have had five penalty attempts, then that team wins the match. Otherwise, the shoot-out continues until one team's penalty score passes the other team's from the same number of attempts.

These players are using a practice penalty shoot-out in training to perfect their penalty skills.

In a shoot-out, each penalty shot has to be taken by a different player, so every member of your team needs to practice.

A practice shoot-out will also improve your goalkeeper's skills.

WINNING A DROP BALL

This page introduces the least common soccer restart, called a drop ball. This is a one-on-one challenge in which a member of each team competes for possession of the ball. To win a drop ball you'll need total concentration and sharp reactions.

DROP BALL BASICS

The referee uses a drop ball to restart play after any stoppage for which neither team is responsible, such as a break in play caused by injury. Unlike other restarts, a drop ball is meant to give both teams an equal chance of gaining possession of the ball.

Two players, one from each team, face one another at the point where the ball was last in play. The referee brings the ball back into play by dropping it onto the field between them. Neither player is allowed to play the ball before it hits the ground.

If your opponents had the ball when the game was interrupted by injury, it is good sportsmanship to let them win it back from the drop ball restart deliberately.

Concentrate on the ball. Try to get your foot to it as soon as it lands.

WINNING WAYS

The simplest approach to a drop ball is to use your instep to tap the ball to a teammate on your nonkicking side.

If you think your opponent will block an instep pass, try using the outside of your foot to hook the ball away to the other side.

You can even try pushing the ball forward through the gap between your opponent's legs. Dodge past him to collect the ball.

CREATING CHANCES

Good dead ball skills will enable you and your team-mates to turn throw-ins, corners, free kicks and penalties into goals. To create as many opportunities as possible to use these skills during a game, you need to put pressure on your opponents so that they send the ball out of play.

PRESSURE PASSING

This cross into the goal area has forced a defender to head the ball out of play.

You can often win a throw-in or corner by passing the ball into a space near your opponents' goal, for a teammate to chase. Your opponents will be forced to clear the ball, rather than allow you a shot at goal.

SHOOTING

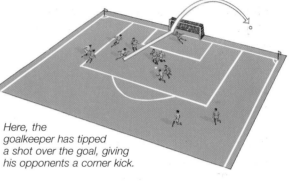

Here, the goalkeeper has tipped a shot over the goal, giving his opponents a corner kick.

Even if you don't score, taking a shot at goal can create a second scoring chance. By blocking your shot, a defender or goalkeeper will often knock the ball out of play to give your team a corner kick.

DRIBBLING INTO ATTACK

Here, the red player's attacking run gains his team a corner kick.

By dribbling into the other team's penalty area, or upfield along either wing, you will often force a defender to try a desperate tackle. In doing so, he may clear the ball for a throw-in or corner, or even give your team a free kick or penalty.

CHALLENGING DEFENDERS

By closing in on a defender, you can force him to play the ball in a hurry.

If one of the other team's players has possession of the ball in his defensive third, move in to challenge him. Under pressure, he is likely to send the ball out of play. This would give your team possession in a good attacking position.

STAR PHOTO

Here, by attacking along the wing, Emmanuel Amunike (Nigeria) forces a defender to clear the ball for a throw-in.

WORLD SOCCER QUIZ

32. Which competition is the oldest international soccer tournament in the world?

a. The European Championship
b. The African Nations Cup
c. The Copa America (South American Championship)

33. Which England striker was the top scorer of the 1986 World Cup?

a. Gary Lineker
b. David Platt
c. Peter Beardsley

34. The first World Cup of the twenty-first century, in 2002, will be hosted by two countries. South Korea is one, what is the other?

a. Japan
b. Malaysia
c. Singapore

35. Which legendary World Cup player has both captained and coached World Cup winning teams?

a. Bobby Charlton
b. Franz Beckenbauer
c. Pele

36. Which World Cup had a stick figure called 'Ciao', with a soccer ball for a head, as its official mascot?

a. 1982, Spain
b. 1986, Mexico
c. 1990, Italy

37. What was special about Dutch player Robbie Rensenbrink's goal against Scotland in 1978?

a. It was fastest goal ever in a World Cup game
b. It was the first time a goalkeeper had scored
c. It was the 1000th World Cup goal

38. Which of these countries has only hosted the World Cup once?

a. Brazil
b. Mexico
c. Italy

39. Which West German striker has scored more World Cup goals than any other player?

a. Uwe Rahn
b. Gerd Müller
c. Karl-Heinz Rummenigge

40. In 1982, Hungary set a new record for the number of goals scored by one team in a World Cup game. How many times did they score?

a. 10
b. 8
c. 6

41. Which of these is the French stadium that was ruled too small to stage the 1998 World Cup Final?

a. Nou Camp
b. Parque Central
c. Parc des Princes

42. Which international team was the first to win the World Cup three times?

a. Argentina
b. Italy
c. Brazil

43. Which country won the 1996 African Nations Cup?

a. Nigeria
b. South Africa
c. Cameroon

44. Which of these international teams does not play in red and white?

a. Croatia
b. Colombia
c. Switzerland

45. Which international soccer confederation does Australia belong to?

a. UEFA
b. CONCACAF
c. Oceania

46. Enzo Francescoli was voted 1995 South American Footballer of the Year. What country does he play for?

a. Uruguay
b. Brazil
c. Colombia

47. Which of these teams did not make it through to the semi-final stages of the 1994 World Cup?

a. Bulgaria
b. Sweden
c. Germany

SOCCER QUIZ
?

PART FOUR
DEFENDING

CONTENTS

ABOUT DEFENDING

When your team loses the ball, you need to get it back as quickly as possible. This is what defending is all about. Defending is every player's responsibility – when the other team has the ball, you are defending, even if you play in an attacking position. A good team defense plays a big part in winning games.

A LOOK AT THE FIELD

Here you can find out the names for different areas of the field mentioned in this part of the book. Although you can defend anywhere on the field, some areas are mentioned more than others because you need to defend more urgently when the other team gets close to your goal.

Good defending is a mixture of individual skills, team skills and tactics. This part of the book covers all of them. It also looks at the roles of players who are specifically defenders, such as center halves and full backs.

The 'far' post is the goal-post farthest from the ball.

The goal area is the box around the goal. The goalkeeper usually tells other players what to do in this area.

Goal line

The penalty area

The 'near' post is the goal post nearest the ball at any time.

Halfway line

THE DEFENSIVE STANCE

When you adopt the 'defensive stance', it is almost like being ready to pounce. You don't have the ball so you don't have to worry about controlling it – you can concentrate on your movements instead.

Use your arms for balance.

You should crouch as low as you can so that you are ready to spring.

Your weight should be over your toes so that you can move quickly into action.

USEFUL SOCCER PHRASES

★ 'Reading the game' means being able to figure out how the game is going, anticipate attackers' moves, see what help your teammates need and go to help them.
★ 'Winning the ball' means taking the ball away from another player by tackling or intercepting it.

AN IMPORTANT RULE: STAYING GOAL-SIDE

One of the main rules for defending players is to get into a goal-side position and stay there. This means placing yourself between attackers and your goal, never between attackers and the ball. This is crucial for successful defending.

Direction of goal

This is the correct direction to take to reach a goal-side position.

If the defender runs to intercept and fails, he gives the attackers a very big advantage.

You may think it makes sense to get between the ball and your opponent, but then you can't see what he's doing.

If he does receive the ball, you have to chase him up the field and he is free to run straight toward your goal.

If you are in a goal-side position, you are able to watch and anticipate the attacker's moves from behind.

Although he is likely to receive the ball successfully, you are in a position to stop his attack and challenge him.

HOW TO MEASURE

For many of the games and exercises in this part of the book, you need to measure out an area to do them in. As before, measurements are given in meters (m) and feet (ft). 1m (3ft) is about one big stride, so you can measure by counting out your strides.

GOAL-SIDE GAME

This game is for two players, an attacker (A) and a defender (D). Mark out a field 20m (66ft) long and 10m (33ft) wide.

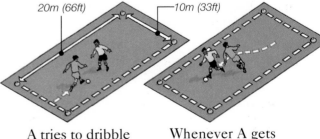

20m (66ft)   10m (33ft)

A tries to dribble down the field. D tries to stop him by staying goal-side, without tackling.

Whenever A gets goal-side of D, he gets a point. At the end, trade roles. See who scores the most.

PRIORITIES IN DEFENSE

The main purpose of a defender or defending team is to stop opponents from attacking. There are many ways to do this, depending on how urgent the situation is. Here, you can find out about the most important things you need to know. They are all covered in detail later in the book.

YOUR TOP PRIORITY

If your opponents reach the defending third, they are in a very strong position. You must stop them from scoring.

First, help your goalkeeper to block any shots at goal. Next, clear the ball out of the danger area – 'if in doubt, get the ball out.'

Here, a defender stops a shot and clears the ball.

DELAYING YOUR OPPONENTS

A very important way of preventing an emergency situation from happening is to delay your opponents as long as possible.

Delay allows members of your own team to get into a stronger position, which may stop the attack from getting any farther.

This player jockeys to give a teammate time to get into position.

CHALLENGING FOR THE BALL

Whatever the situation, someone must try to win the ball back. This responsibility passes from player to player, so everyone must be ready to take on the challenge if the ball comes his way.

Attacker   *Defender*

You can challenge by putting pressure on the player with the ball.

If your opponent makes a mistake, you or a team-mate can intercept the ball.

As a last resort, you can challenge your opponent directly with a tackle.

AWARENESS AND TEAM WORK

Even if one player's skills are very good, he will not stand a very big chance of challenging for the ball successfully if his team is not working with him.

Each player has a part to play in making it difficult for the other team to progress up the field. To do this you need to communicate well.

Everyone needs to be aware of where the ball is, but not everyone should crowd around it.

All players should be aware of what the attackers are doing, especially the players they are marking.

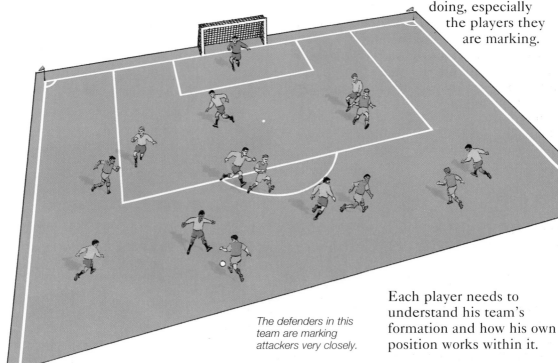

The defenders in this team are marking attackers very closely.

Each player needs to understand his team's formation and how his own position works within it.

DEFENSE INTO ATTACK

If you only think about stopping the other team from scoring, you are less likely to score yourself. A good defense makes the whole team strong, but it should always be used as a springboard for attack.

Think positively all the time so that you can turn defensive situations into an attack as soon as you get the chance.

This team gains possession in the defending third, then sends the ball quickly up the field.

STAR DEFENDER

German player Dieter Eilts is a good example of a defender who can read the game well, then play fearlessly to turn defense into attack.

JOCKEYING

Jockeying is one of the most important defending skills. It means delaying your opponent's attack by getting in his way. This allows your teammates to get into a position where they can help you to challenge. If you do this effectively, you may also pressure your opponent into making a mistake.

MOVING INTO POSITION

If your opponent is approaching your goal, you need to close in on him quickly, but not too quickly. If you are going too fast he will be able to judge your run and go around you easily.

The defender watches the ball carefully.

Direction of goal

Once you are close to the attacker, hold off slightly. You should be close enough to touch him, but if you get much closer it will be easy for him to go around you.

Adopt the 'defensive stance'. If your weight is over your knees, you are in a strong position to challenge.

Make sure you stay goal-side. If the attacker gets past you, he has beaten you. You will no longer be able to jockey.

MAINTAINING THE PRESSURE

As well as delaying your opponent, try to force him into a weaker position. First of all, try to figure out which is his weaker side – if he usually uses his right foot to dribble or kick, he is weak on his left side.

This player jockeys on the left.

Cover your opponent to the front and to one side so that it is difficult for him to turn.

The attacker is forced into the sideline.

If you jockey on his strong side, he will only be able to use his weak side, so he may make a mistake.

Here, the attacker loses the initiative.

Once you have your opponent under pressure, watch for opportunities to win the ball.

PREVENTING A FULL TURN

If the attacker is still facing away from your goal when you reach a jockeying position, you have a big advantage. The best thing you can do is prevent him from turning.

1. Jockey on his stronger side, getting close up behind him. You must stay goal-side, so don't come around to his front.

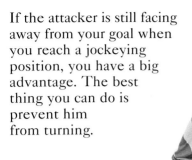

Direction of goal

Direction of goal

2. If you prevent him from turning like this, you will probably force him to pass the ball back.

Direction of goal

3. If he passes back, he may turn and run into space behind you. Stick with him and stay goal-side.

ZIGZAG JOCKEYING EXERCISE

This exercise helps you to work on speed and a good defensive stance. Any number can join in, as long as you work in pairs. Mark out a row of zigzags about 30m (98ft) long and 5m (16ft) wide. One end of the row is the defender's goal. In each pair, decide on an attacker and a defender.

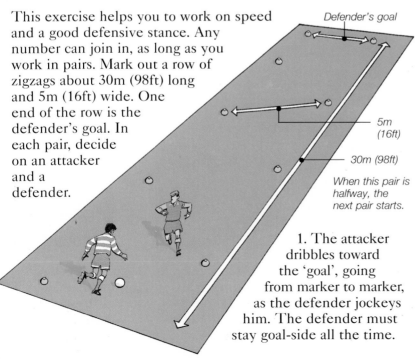

Defender's goal

5m (16ft)

30m (98ft)

When this pair is halfway, the next pair starts.

1. The attacker dribbles toward the 'goal', going from marker to marker, as the defender jockeys him. The defender must stay goal-side all the time.

2. The defender can't tackle, but he scores a point for intercepting the ball if the attacker loses control. The attacker scores if he goes around the defender. At the end of the row, trade roles and start again.

CHALLENGING

When you challenge, you make a direct attempt to get the ball back from your opponents. The most direct way to challenge is to tackle, but it is not always the best. If you can, intercept the ball because this will leave you with more control.

Defender

APPROACHING AN OPPONENT

You usually move in to challenge when your opponent is about to receive a pass. Always get into a goal-side position.

The defender should not run right to the back of his opponent in the direction of the curved arrow.

Approach your opponent at an angle. If you are directly behind him, he can easily run out to the side.

Don't get in too close to him, as he may be able to move around you.

Judge your speed carefully. If you come in slowly he may run past you. If you are too fast, you have less control.

This defender has come in too fast and too close. He is off balance.

If the defender approaches in this direction, he will be able to challenge the attacker.

Direction of goal

INTERCEPTING

Intercepting is the best way to win the ball back. Your opponents are usually moving in the wrong direction, and you are more balanced than if you tackle. This means that you have the time and space to launch an attack.

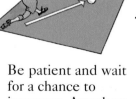

Be patient and wait for a chance to intercept. Attackers may make mistakes under pressure.

You must be on your toes and ready to go around your opponent from your goal-side position.

Wait, then intercept later.

If you don't think you can intercept successfully, stay in your goal-side position instead.

TIMING A DIRECT CHALLENGE

If you are close to your opponent, you will probably need to tackle in order to win the ball. In judging your tackle, the most important factor is timing.

One of the main rules of timing is to watch the ball, not the player. This way, you won't be fooled by his movements. Wait until he is off balance, for example when he is turning or half-turned, then move in quickly to steal the ball. You can find out more about tackling techniques on pages 106-107.

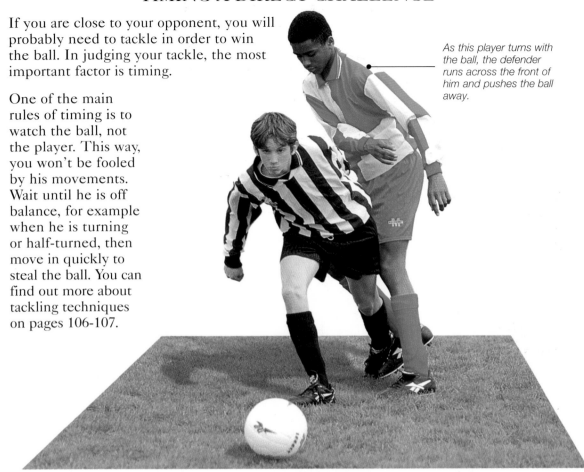

As this player turns with the ball, the defender runs across the front of him and pushes the ball away.

INTERCEPTING EXERCISE

This exercise is to help you develop your agility and speed at intercepting. Play in threes (A, B and D). Mark out a 10m (33ft) square. A and D stand in the middle of it, B along one edge. The direction of play is toward A and D.

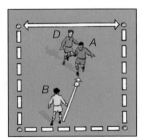

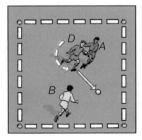

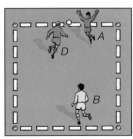

D stands goal-side of A. B passes toward them. D must judge whether to intercept or stay goal-side.

If D intercepts, he scores a point and passes the ball back to B before A can challenge him.

If A gets the ball, D tries to stop him reaching the far side of the square before B can count to ten.

A scores a point for turning and reaching the other side. When he has had five turns, trade roles.

TACKLING SKILLS

To tackle well you need a combination of good technique and plenty of determination. You need to tackle cleanly to avoid fouling, and whenever possible you need to keep possession of the ball, too. These are the main techniques that you need to learn.

FRONT BLOCK TACKLE

Watch the ball, not your opponent. With your weight forward, go into the tackle with your whole body.

Use the inside of your tackling foot to make contact with the middle of the ball.

If you watch your opponent instead of the ball, you may be tricked by a faking move.

The impact of the tackle can often trap the ball between your foot and your opponent's foot. If this happens, drop your foot down and try to flick or roll the ball up over your opponent's foot.

TACKLING FROM OTHER ANGLES

You can use a block tackle to challenge from the side, but not from behind as this is a foul.

Turn your whole body toward your opponent so that all your strength is behind the tackle. Use the side of your tackling foot as you would if you were head on. Lean into your opponent, but don't push.

BLOCK TACKLE PRACTICE

In pairs, mark out a 10m (33ft) line. Start at either end. One player dribbles, the other challenges.

10m (33ft)

The dribbler tries to get to the end of the line, while the challenger tries to win the ball from him. Whoever succeeds scores a point.

SLIDE TACKLES

Slide tackles are a last resort. You should only use them in a real emergency, for several reasons. You will probably not gain possession of the ball, you are out of the game until you get up again, and you may also be called for a foul.

Approach from the side. Keep your eyes on the ball and slide your tackling leg forward to push the ball as far as possible.

This player uses the leg farthest from his opponent to hook the ball away from him.

If you kick the ball and not your opponent, you will not be penalized if he has to jump over you.

After tackling, get up quickly. This is easier if you tackle with the leg farthest from your opponent.

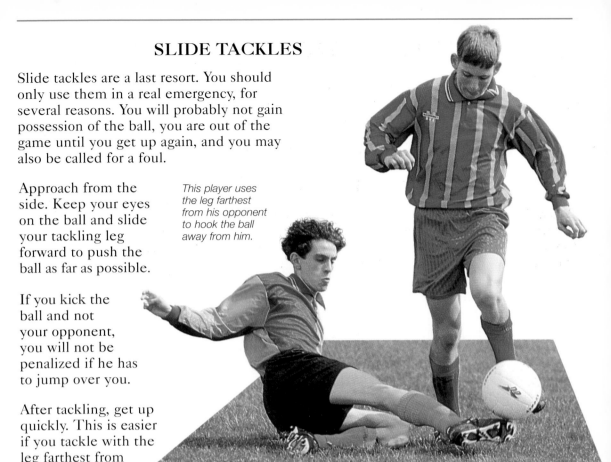

LEARNING TO SLIDE TACKLE

Until you are sure of your technique, it is best to practice slide tackles without an opponent, as you are less likely to hurt someone. Try this practice with a friend.

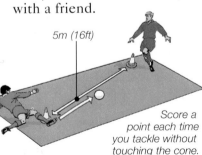

5m (16ft)

Score a point each time you tackle without touching the cone.

Place two obstacles 5m (16ft) apart and put the ball close to one of them. These are your 'opponents'. Each of you starts by standing next to an obstacle.

One of you runs up and slides the ball away, trying not to touch the obstacle. The other collects the ball and puts it next to his own obstacle. He slides it back.

KEEPING IT CLEAN

Tackling your opponent from behind, kicking him or tripping him are fouls which lead to a direct free kick, or a penalty if you are in the penalty area. To avoid fouling, remember these tips:
★ Keep your eyes on the ball, not on your opponent.
★ Be patient. If you wait for the right moment to tackle, you are more likely to do so cleanly.
★ Never tackle half-heartedly. If your weight is not behind the tackle, you may be unbalanced, and you could hurt yourself as well as your opponent.

PLAYING SAFE

Usually, you are defending whenever your team loses the ball. However, when the ball is in your defending third, you may need to play defensively even when your team has possession.

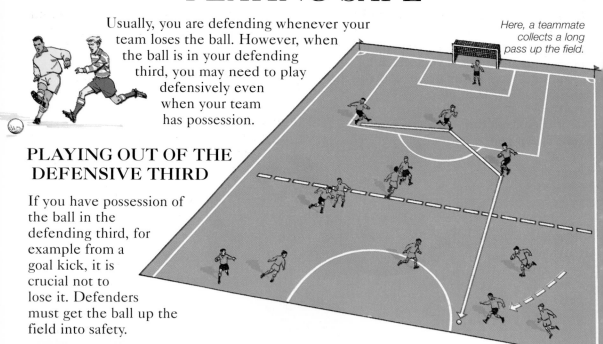

Here, a teammate collects a long pass up the field.

PLAYING OUT OF THE DEFENSIVE THIRD

If you have possession of the ball in the defending third, for example from a goal kick, it is crucial not to lose it. Defenders must get the ball up the field into safety.

Never dribble out of the defending third. Any attacker who wins the ball may be able to shoot.

This attacker wins the ball and can now go for goal.

You can pass between yourselves at the back until you get a good opportunity to pass up the field.

When you pass up the field, send the ball as far as you can, to a teammate if possible.

BACK-PASSES

A 'back-pass' usually means passing the ball back to the goalkeeper. If you want to pass up the field but find yourself surrounded, this is sometimes your only option.

1. Never pass across your goalmouth, as this may give your opponents a chance to run in and shoot.

2. Don't pass back to the goalkeeper if he is under pressure. It is better to kick the ball out of play.

3. Play the ball low, to the goalkeeper's kicking foot. This makes it easier for him to control.

BACK-PASS RULES

There are particular rules for back-passes to bear in mind.
★ If you kick the ball to him, the goalkeeper can't pick it up. He has to kick it instead.
★ The goalkeeper can pick up any back-pass that you make with your head, chest or thighs.
★ The goalkeeper can pick up any accidental back-pass.

CLEARING OUT OF BOUNDS

Clearing out of bounds means sending the ball off the field on purpose as an emergency move. The other team still has the initiative because they get the corner or throw-in, but it can stop them from scoring while your team uses the time to strengthen its position.

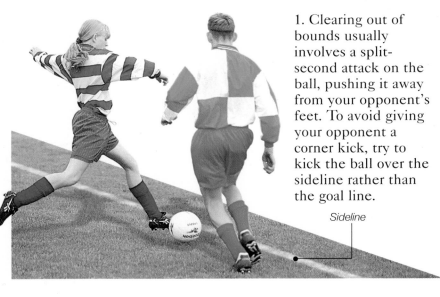

1. Clearing out of bounds usually involves a split-second attack on the ball, pushing it away from your opponent's feet. To avoid giving your opponent a corner kick, try to kick the ball over the sideline rather than the goal line.

Sideline

Here, a throw-in gives defenders time.

2. If you have cleared out of bounds, your whole team must use the time you have gained to run into a stronger position.

THE PENALTY AREA: GETTING INTO POSITION

In your penalty area, you should do everything you can to prevent a goal, but don't take any risks.

Keep a close guard on other attackers close to the penalty area.

Help your goalkeeper by listening to him carefully.

This player jockeys while other defenders get into position.

Position yourself to stop any shots, as this player is doing.

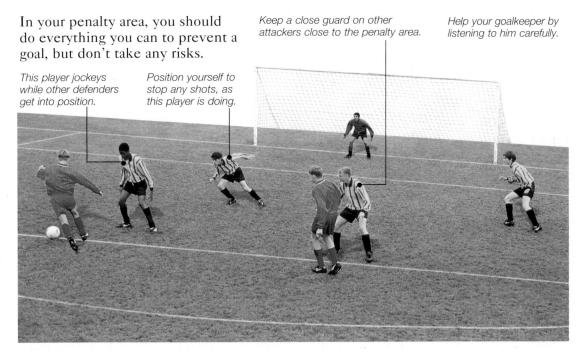

You should still try to delay your opponent for as long as possible.

Don't try to tackle the player with the ball unless you are sure of success.

Help the goalkeeper by getting into a position to block any shots at goal.

If you get to kick the ball, make sure you clear it out of danger (see page 110).

CLEARING THE BALL

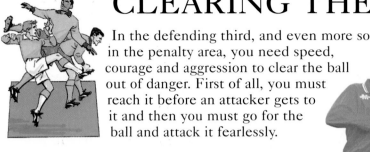

In the defending third, and even more so in the penalty area, you need speed, courage and aggression to clear the ball out of danger. First of all, you must reach it before an attacker gets to it and then you must go for the ball and attack it fearlessly.

SPEED, HEIGHT AND DISTANCE

Volleys are good for sending the ball high.

You must get to the ball quickly. When you get to it, aim for the wings. Attackers are more likely to come up the center of the field.

Send the ball as high as you can. This gives your team time to get into position, even if it doesn't go very far.

It is even better to send the ball high and a long way. Use a powerful kick such as a lofted drive to get height and distance.

DEFENSIVE HEADERS

As for any header, keep your mouth shut and your eyes open.

Take the ball as early as possible. This will automatically send your header higher and farther.

Brace your legs and take off on one leg, springing at the ball and arching your back in the air.

Try to hit the ball from underneath so that your forehead sends it high over attackers' heads.

If you need to, turn your head as you make contact to send the ball away from the penalty area.

CLASHES IN THE AIR

The penalty area is often crowded, so clashes with attackers in the air are bound to happen. Success in this situation requires courage and dominance, so take the initiative. Attacking the ball aggressively actually gives you greater control.

Communicate with your goalkeeper and team-mates to avoid clashing with them as well as with attackers.

Timing is crucial. Try to jump before the attacker. He may then push you up farther from underneath.

Be careful not to be called for a foul. Don't push the attacker with your arms.

STAR HEADER

When you watch professional players, see how they approach the ball in the penalty area. You will see that they are never afraid to leap into the air and go for the ball, and they are not afraid of making physical contact with other players.

Here, Spanish midfielder 'Felipe' Minambres leaps for the ball in a match against Korea.

CLEARANCE PRACTICE

This practice is best for seven players in the positions shown, but you can vary it. The two Ws stand on either side of the penalty area and everyone else in the goalmouth.

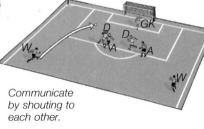

Communicate by shouting to each other.

One of the Ws sends a high pass into the goalmouth. The GK and Ds have to communicate quickly and decide who will go for it.

If a D gets to the ball, he should try to direct it out to a W with a header, lofted drive or volley. If an A gets to the ball, he tries to shoot.

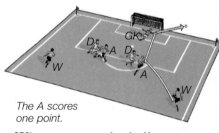

The A scores one point.

Whoever gets the ball first scores a point. Ds score two for getting the ball out of the penalty area, As two for scoring. Trade roles after five passes.

SUPPORT PLAY

Individual defending skills are very important, but in order to win games you must also work well as a team. While one player challenges for the ball, everyone else should try to stop other attackers from getting into a strong position.

Here, one player challenges while the others close down on opponents.

CLOSING DOWN SPACE

Your opponents will try to spread the game out and make holes in your defense by running into space. 'Closing down space' means moving to cover attackers who are free, while one or two players move in to cover the player with the ball.

Direction of goal

Everyone should run into a goal-side position. Make sure you cover all the players who are likely to receive a pass.

Try to move up the field together. Working well with each other makes it much harder for attackers to find space in between you.

The result should be that the attackers' route is blocked, and that they have nowhere to pass the ball.

COVERING A CHALLENGE

If you are close to a player challenging for the ball, you must give him all the help you can to stop the attack. If the attacker gets past him, you should be ready to take up the challenge. Here, you can see a two-on-two situation where two defenders mark two attackers.

As one attacker (A1) passes to the other (A2), one defender (D1) moves in to challenge him.

The other defender (D2) moves back at an angle so that he can still keep an eye on A1.

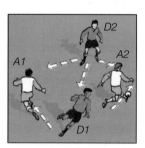

D1 now has cover behind him if he loses the challenge, but A1 is still being marked by D2.

MARKING

Good marking is one of the keys to a solid defense. When and who you mark may depend on your marking system (see pages 114-115) but the basic principles stay the same.

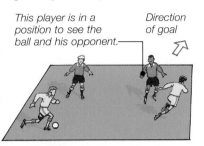

This player is in a position to see the ball and his opponent.

Direction of goal

You need to be goal-side and at the correct angle from your opponent so that you can watch him and the game at the same time.

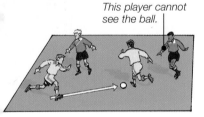

This player cannot see the ball.

If you mark directly behind your opponent, you may block your own view of the game. It is also difficult to intercept any passes to him.

This attacker manages to get around the defense.

If you turn to watch the ball without keeping an eye on the player you are marking, he may be able to sneak around you.

JUDGING YOUR DISTANCE

To judge the right distance to keep, figure out how fast your opponent is. Do this by watching him carefully at the start of the game. If he is slower than you, stay fairly close to him. You may be able to intercept passes coming his way.

By marking tightly, this defender can move around the attacker.

If your opponent is faster than you, stay at about arm's length from him. If you get too close, he may be able to go around you when he receives the ball.

This defender is ready to challenge.

MARKING SYSTEMS

A marking system is a way of organizing your team so that everyone knows who should be covering which attacker. These are the systems used most often, which can be adapted to fit the strengths and weaknesses of your team.

MAN-TO-MAN MARKING

When your team marks man-to-man, a specific defender marks each of the attackers from the other team. They watch this attacker throughout the game and stay goal-side of him whenever necessary.

Here, the defenders are moving into position.

Playing man-to-man works well in the defending third, as long as you have some extra defenders to put the attackers under pressure. Never let just one player mark the opponent who has the ball.

As the play moves across the field toward the penalty area, the marking defenders stay with the same player, keeping goal-side and marking tightly. This makes it difficult for the attackers to shoot.

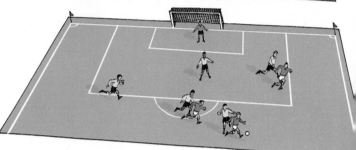

ZONAL MARKING

In zonal marking, you are responsible for an area or zone instead of one player. This area depends on the position you are playing, but not too strictly. As you move up and down the field, your area moves with you. Usually, you mark anyone who comes within 5-10m (16-33ft) of you.

In this example of how the zonal system works, an attacker (A) moves across the defense.

D1 covers the player until he moves out of his area, when D2 covers him instead.

The advantage of this is that D1 has not left a big space behind him for attackers to fill.

MIXING SYSTEMS

Many professional teams don't work with just one system. Often, they mix different systems to make the most of their skills. This takes a lot of discipline and organization to put into practice effectively.

When one player in the other team is very skilled, one defender might mark him man-to-man while the others mark zonally, as this picture shows.

Some teams play zonally in the attacking third and midfield, then use a man-to-man system in defense.

One defender marks this fast winger closely, while the other defenders mark zonally.

You can also mark different players at different times as a looser man-to-man system.

USING A SWEEPER

Whichever system you use, it is too risky to allow a one-on-one situation to develop in the defending third. To stop this from happening, you can use a 'sweeper', who doesn't mark anyone (see pages 116-117). He stays at the back and 'sweeps up' attackers who get past the main defense.

FINDING THE BEST SYSTEM

There is no 'best system' which works for every team in every situation. These are the factors which are important.

★ Whatever system you use, the whole team must fully understand it. Each player must know exactly what he is supposed to do.

★ Try to find out about your opponents and about their strengths and weaknesses. If they have some good players, make sure they are well marked.

★ Think about the skills of your own team – for example, you might put a row of strong players to mark zonally at the back, and you wouldn't place a weak player man-to-man against a strong opponent.

This sweeper gets into a good position to challenge an attacker who has broken through the defense.

Direction of goal

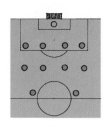

TEAM FORMATIONS

Along with a marking system, each professional team has a formation. A formation is almost like a map of the positions that the players stick to during the game. It can be different each time a team plays, though teams often use the one they feel most confident with.

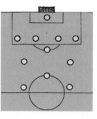

HOW IS A FORMATION BUILT?

A strong formation always has a strong defense. A team is usually built up solidly with a strong group of defenders at the back for the attacking forwards to rely upon. The idea is that if the other team can't score, they can't win. This way of thinking, however, can lead to play that is too defensive and to games which end in a tie. To win, the midfield and forwards need the support and freedom to push forward and score, so modern formations are also designed for this.

FOUR-FOUR-TWO

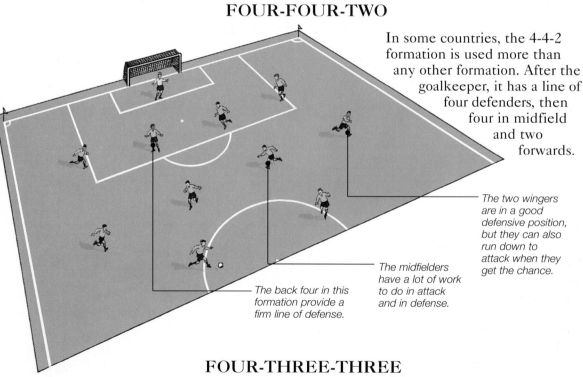

In some countries, the 4-4-2 formation is used more than any other formation. After the goalkeeper, it has a line of four defenders, then four in midfield and two forwards.

The two wingers are in a good defensive position, but they can also run down to attack when they get the chance.

The midfielders have a lot of work to do in attack and in defense.

The back four in this formation provide a firm line of defense.

FOUR-THREE-THREE

This formation is similar to the 4-4-2 formation. It has a goalkeeper, four defenders, three midfielders and three forwards. The advantage of this is that there is more emphasis on attack, but the problem can be that the midfield is not strong enough to push the ball forward in the first place.

Having less midfielders makes the defense weaker.

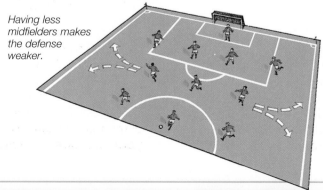

THE SWEEPER FORMATION

Using a sweeper changes a formation at the back. Traditionally, the system is based on a five-man defense. The usual line of four is backed up by a 'spare' man or sweeper.

This formation gives a very secure defense. However, with so many players at the back, a team using it may find it difficult to attack.

Another version has more players in attack. It uses the usual back four, but one player drops back when necessary to play sweeper.

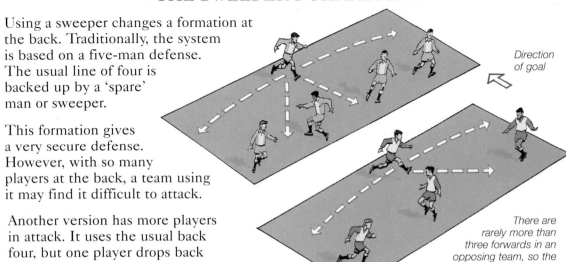

Direction of goal

There are rarely more than three forwards in an opposing team, so the sweeper is still a 'spare' player.

OTHER FORMATIONS

There are many other combinations which teams can try. This is an example. It is based on the 4-4-2 formation, but it is a lot more flexible.

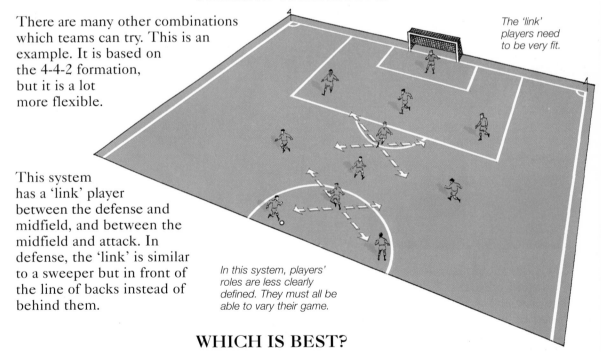

The 'link' players need to be very fit.

This system has a 'link' player between the defense and midfield, and between the midfield and attack. In defense, the 'link' is similar to a sweeper but in front of the line of backs instead of behind them.

In this system, players' roles are less clearly defined. They must all be able to vary their game.

WHICH IS BEST?

Each formation has its advantages and teams tend to get used to playing in one way. Many European teams, for example, use a sweeper. The following factors make a difference when you are deciding which to use.

★ Don't try to fit players to a formation which doesn't suit them. Choose one which suits their skills.
★ If you use a very traditional formation, your game may be too easy for your opponents to read.

★ If you use a new, flexible formation, you must all be able to read the game well, and you must also be very fit.
★ Make sure you have a strong defense. If it is weak, you may lose even if your forwards are good.

THE OFFSIDES RULE

The offsides rule can sometimes be very useful for defenders, as attackers who are caught in this position have an indirect free kick awarded against them. Here you can find out about how the rule works and the best way for defenders to use it.

OFFSIDES

To be penalized for offsides, an attacker must be in your half of the field and there must be fewer than two defenders between him and the goal line. One of these defenders can be the goalkeeper. It is not always illegal to be offsides, but it is in any of these cases:

1. A player can only be called offsides when the ball is played, not when it is received.

2. Offsides should be called if a player's offsides position gives him an advantage, for example a chance to shoot.

3. If a player is offsides and obstructs a defender to stop him from reaching the ball, he should be penalized.

LEGAL POSITIONS

An attacker will not be penalized for offsides in any of these situations:

1. If one of the last defenders is level with him when the ball is passed. To be offsides he must be closer to the goal line.

2. If he receives the ball directly from a goal kick, corner or throw-in. If he receives it indirectly, he is offsides.

3. If he runs into an offsides position after the ball has been played, or if he dribbles into an offsides position.

4. If he is offsides, but not interfering with play at all – for example, if he is on the other side of the field or if he is lying injured.

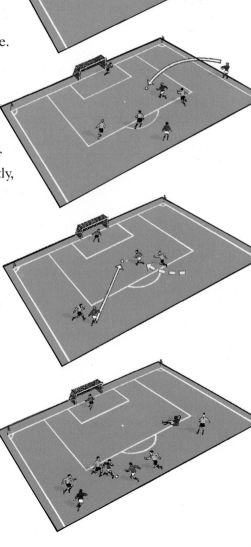

USING OFFSIDES IN DEFENSE

You may see professional defenders trying to place an attacker offsides by moving up the field together, just at the point when another attacker passes to him. Here you can see how this 'trap' works.

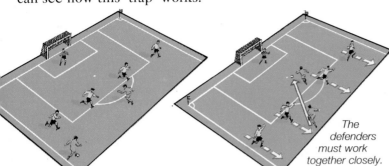

The back line of defenders see that an attacker is about to receive a pass.

They all move up the field just before or just as the pass is made.

The defenders must work together closely.

DISADVANTAGES OF USING OFFSIDES

A big problem with using offsides is that you depend upon the referee. If he does not call offsides, you leave your defense in a very weak position. Also, the trap may not work. If an attacker manages to dribble past you instead of passing, he can go straight for goal.

OFFSIDES QUIZ

Which of these situations show a player in an offsides position? Think carefully before you decide. The answers are on page 130.

1.

2.

3.

4.

This attacker fools the defense by dribbling past them instead of passing.

The defenders expect the ball to be passed to this player.

The defenders have all moved up, so it will be difficult for them to help the goalkeeper defend against the attacker.

DEFENSIVE POSITIONS

Some particular positions, such as center half and full back, are more defensive than others, and require special skills. Here you can find out about the skills needed by players in the midfield and at the back.

PLAYING CENTER HALF

The center half's number one job is to stop the other team from scoring.

★ You must not be afraid to challenge for the ball and tackle. It helps if you are strong.

★ You need to be able to head the ball well.

★ You need to read the game from the back and communicate well with your teammates.

★ If you move forward when your team attacks, you must be able to move goal-side quickly if your opponents counter-attack.

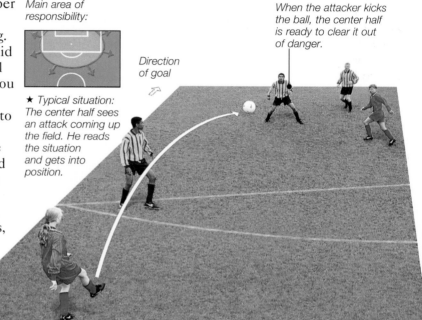

Main area of responsibility:

★ Typical situation: The center half sees an attack coming up the field. He reads the situation and gets into position.

Direction of goal

When the attacker kicks the ball, the center half is ready to clear it out of danger.

PLAYING SWEEPER

In some formations, a center half drops back to play sweeper (see page 117), so the skills needed are similar. These are the main differences:

★ You have to cover the whole of the area behind the back four, so you must be quick and agile.

★ You must be an even better judge of the game, as you are farther back than a center half and in a position to spot any danger.

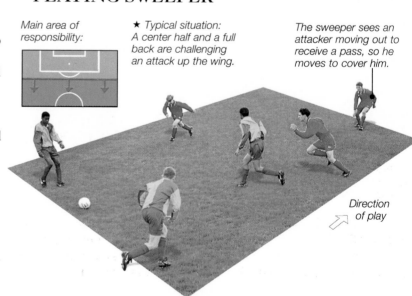

Main area of responsibility:

★ Typical situation: A center half and a full back are challenging an attack up the wing.

The sweeper sees an attacker moving out to receive a pass, so he moves to cover him.

Direction of play

PLAYING FULL BACK

A full back plays in defense, but on the wing. This is a varied role. You need lots of different skills to play it well.

★ Like a center half, you need to be aggressive and strong to clear the ball out of danger.

★ Because you are on the wing, you need to be fast, fit and able to make runs up and down the field to support the attack as well as the defense.

★ You need to be good at jockeying attackers on the wing to give other defenders time to get into position.

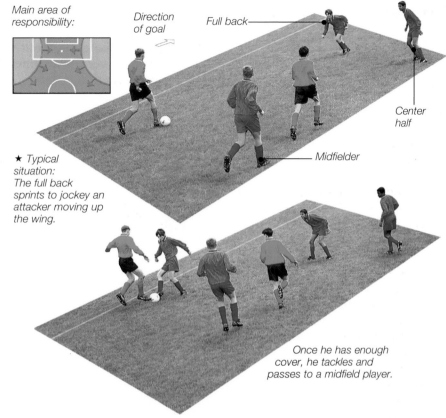

Main area of responsibility:

Direction of goal

Full back

Center half

Midfielder

★ Typical situation: The full back sprints to jockey an attacker moving up the wing.

Once he has enough cover, he tackles and passes to a midfield player.

PLAYING IN MIDFIELD

Midfield players need to be all-around players. They have to support the defense when needed, but they must also be good in attack. 'Anchors' and 'wing backs' are two kinds of midfielder with particular roles in defense.

Main area of responsibility for wing backs:

★ Typical situation: The wing back works with a full back in the early stages of an attack.

Together they close down space around the attacker.

Main area of responsibility for anchor:

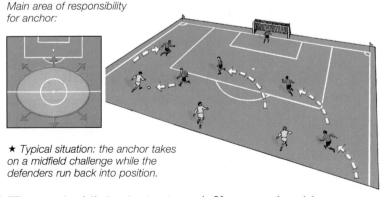

★ Typical situation: the anchor takes on a midfield challenge while the defenders run back into position.

The 'anchor' links the backs and midfield players.
★ You must be able to jockey, challenge and attack.

★ You must be able to read the game in front and behind you and give support wherever it is needed.

Wing backs help challenge attacks on the wing.
★ You must be good at covering for defenders and giving support.
★ You must be fit and fast and be a good dribbler.

CORNER KICKS

A corner kick is one of the most dangerous situations for a defending team. Your opponents have a high chance of scoring, so you need to be clear about what each player is going to do and be very disciplined in carrying out your tactics.

KEY POSITIONS

Think about what your opponents might try. Some moves are often used. One is swinging the ball in close to the near post, and another is swinging it out for a key attacker to head at goal. Prepare by placing your best players in the danger areas.

One reliable defender should support the goalkeeper by covering the far post.

The goalkeeper should stand in front of the far post to see the goal and penalty area.

One defender should cover the near post, but without blocking the goalkeeper's view.

Attackers often aim for the near post because it is hard for the goalkeeper to reach.

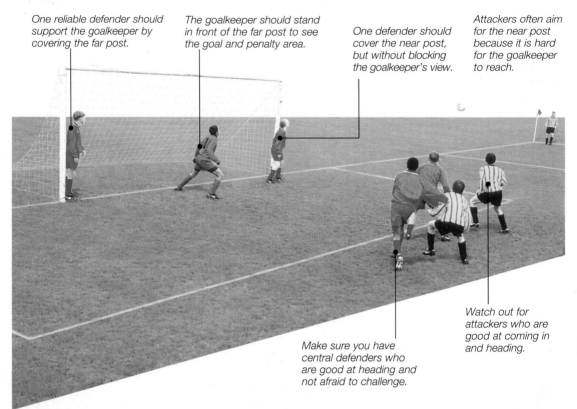

Make sure you have central defenders who are good at heading and not afraid to challenge.

Watch out for attackers who are good at coming in and heading.

CORNER RULES

There are two main rules which make a difference to defending at a corner:
★ Remember that an attacker cannot be offsides from a direct corner kick.
★ All defenders have to keep a distance of 9m (30ft) from the player taking the corner.

HELPING THE GOALKEEPER

The goalkeeper is in charge of the goal area during a corner kick, so listen for his instructions and don't block his view. This is very important around the near post and goal area.

Here, Belgian goalkeeper Michel Preud'homme reaches for the ball in a match against Morocco.

COVERING SHORT CORNERS

If you see an attacker moving out toward the player taking the corner kick, your opponents may try a 'short corner'. By making a short pass to another attacker they get a different angle of approach to the goal, and they hope to take your team by surprise.

Two of you can stop this attack by moving forward. Remember the 9m (30ft) rule. You need two players because the player taking the corner kick will move out as soon as he has done so.

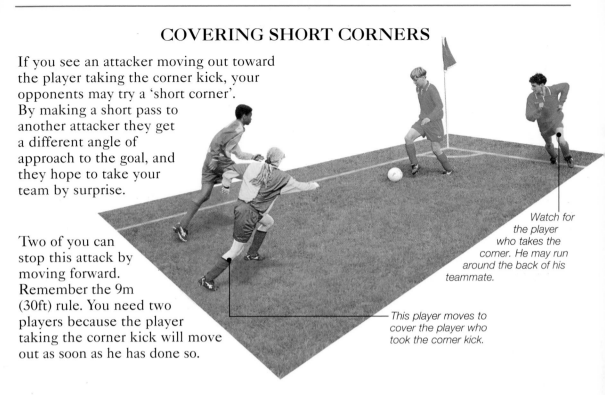

Watch for the player who takes the corner. He may run around the back of his teammate.

This player moves to cover the player who took the corner kick.

FILLING IN THE GAPS

Once the key positions are covered, the rest of you must make sure there are no other holes. How you do this will depend on which marking system you use.

If you are marking zonally, the team spreads out evenly over the penalty area. Each player should cover the area in front of him.

In a real situation, there would be many more attackers in the areas filled by the arrows.

If you are marking man-to-man, you should get goal-side of your opponent and stick with him as he tries to find space to run into.

The attackers may use most of their players.

ATTACKING THE BALL

When you are all in place and the corner kick is taken, you must all stay alert and make sure you are first to the ball to get it out of danger. As long as you challenge fairly, you don't need to worry about bumping into other players.

Here, Gareth Southgate and Paul Ince, playing in the England team, challenge for the ball together in a match against Switzerland.

FREE KICKS AND THROW-INS

Any dead ball situation that is awarded against you gives your opponents an advantage. Having gained possession, they will try to create good shooting opportunities, especially in your defending third. You need to stay alert and disciplined.

As the throw is taken, defenders move into goal-side positions.

DEFENDING AT THROW-INS

This player is not offsides. A player cannot be offsides from a direct throw-in.

Your opponents will take the throw-in as quickly as they can, so don't lose your concentration and don't stop moving. Use the time to move into a stronger goal-side position.

Mark any player who is likely to receive the throw. Someone should mark the thrower so that he can't run into space after the throw.

Treat long throws in the defending third like corner kicks (see pages 122-123).

INDIRECT FREE KICKS

When an indirect free kick is awarded against you, you must go back 9m (30ft) from the ball. Your opponents cannot shoot directly at goal – another player has to touch the ball first. This means that as soon as the kick is taken, you can move in to close down the gap before an opponent shoots.

In or near the penalty area you can form a wall (see opposite). Be ready to move very quickly.

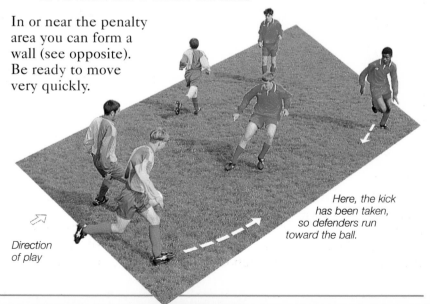

Direction of play

Here, the kick has been taken, so defenders run toward the ball.

DIRECT FREE KICKS

A direct free kick allows opponents a direct shot at goal. In your defensive third, you need a defensive wall to block the shot. This should cover as much of the goal as possible without blocking the goalkeeper's view, and must be 9m (30ft) from the kick. You should also move plenty of other players into the penalty area.

BUILDING A WALL

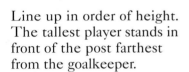

Watch the ball by lifting your eyes, not your head.

You must form the wall quickly.

Line up in order of height. The tallest player stands in front of the post farthest from the goalkeeper.

Everyone in the wall should stand very close to the player next to him so that there aren't any gaps.

Protect your head by tucking it down on your chest, and place your hands over your genitals.

CENTRAL KICKS

If the kick is in front of the goal, you will need up to five players in the wall. Line up so that the goalkeeper has a view of the ball.

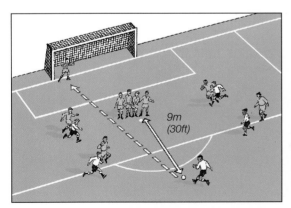

9m (30ft)

Other players should mark attackers man-to-man, but also keep a good view of the ball.

The wall must hold firm as the kick is taken, then move quickly to follow up any rebounds.

KICKS FROM THE SIDE

If the kick is to the side of the goal, it is more likely that the kicker will try to cross the ball to another attacker.

9m (30ft)

Here, you only need two or three players in the wall. The rest of you should spread out.

As soon as the kick is taken, everyone must move toward the ball quickly to clear it out of danger.

DEFENSE INTO ATTACK

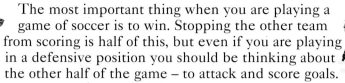

The most important thing when you are playing a game of soccer is to win. Stopping the other team from scoring is half of this, but even if you are playing in a defensive position you should be thinking about the other half of the game – to attack and score goals.

GETTING AN OVERVIEW

Your overall attitude when you are in defense is essential for your success. If your team falls apart as soon as you lose possession, the other team will probably win. Always believe that you can win the ball back, and be ready to attack again.

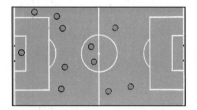

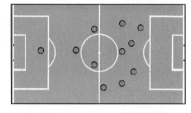

1. This team is in a weak position. It is spread out, leaving lots of holes. This makes it difficult to work together and push forward.

2. This team is in a much stronger position. Although it is in its defending third, the team can communicate and send the ball forward.

3. This team is in a strong position, too. Although there is a lot of space behind the defense, the attackers will find it hard to move into it.

DEFENDING FROM THE BACK

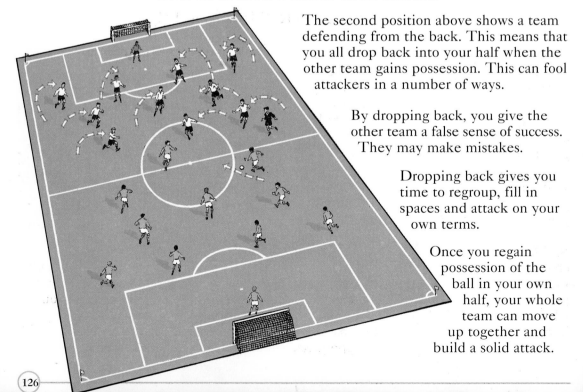

The second position above shows a team defending from the back. This means that you all drop back into your half when the other team gains possession. This can fool attackers in a number of ways.

By dropping back, you give the other team a false sense of success. They may make mistakes.

Dropping back gives you time to regroup, fill in spaces and attack on your own terms.

Once you regain possession of the ball in your own half, your whole team can move up together and build a solid attack.

DEFENDING FROM THE FRONT

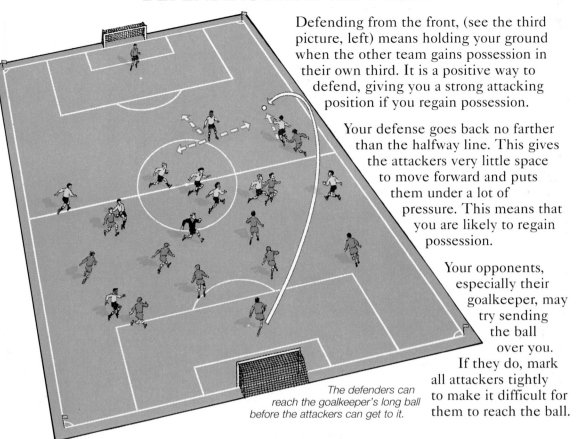

Defending from the front, (see the third picture, left) means holding your ground when the other team gains possession in their own third. It is a positive way to defend, giving you a strong attacking position if you regain possession.

Your defense goes back no farther than the halfway line. This gives the attackers very little space to move forward and puts them under a lot of pressure. This means that you are likely to regain possession.

Your opponents, especially their goalkeeper, may try sending the ball over you. If they do, mark all attackers tightly to make it difficult for them to reach the ball.

The defenders can reach the goalkeeper's long ball before the attackers can get to it.

SUMMARY AND REMINDER TIPS

★ Always stay in a goal-side position from your opponent.

★ Delay your opponents as much as you can by jockeying.

★ Watch your man when you are marking. Don't let yourself be distracted.

★ When challenging for the ball, put your whole body into it.

★ Learn to clear the ball with strong headers and lofted drives.

★ Play wisely in your defending third. Don't take silly risks.

★ Concentrate when the ball goes out of play. Use the time to get into position.

★ As a team, close down the space and options open to opponents.

★ Make sure you understand your team formation and your position in it.

★ Above all, think positively and keep working as a team, so that when you gain possession you are in a strong position to launch an attack.

WORLD SOCCER QUIZ

48. Which of these countries won the 1996 European Championship?

a. Czech Republic
b. Germany
c. France

49. Which World Cup had a smiling green chili called 'Pique' as its official mascot?

a. 1982, Spain
b. 1986, Mexico
c. 1990, Italy

50. Which country was successful in its bid to host the 1998 World Cup?

a. Russia
b. Brazil
c. France

51. Who beat Brazil in the 1996 Olympics to win the gold medal?

a. Nigeria
b. France
c. Argentina

52. Which English player scored the only ever hat trick in a World Cup Final?

a. Geoff Hurst
b. Bobby Charlton
c. Nobby Stiles

53. In 1958, Brazilian legend Pele became the youngest player ever to play in a World Cup Final. How old was he?

a. 16
b. 17
c. 19

54. Why was Argentinian star Diego Maradona banned from the 1994 World Cup?

a. He used his hands to score a goal
b. He hit a referee
c. He failed a drugs test

55. In 1958, French striker Just Fontaine set a new record for the most goals in a World Cup tournament. How many did he score?

a. 6
b. 13
c. 10

56. What color uniform do the Brazilian national team usually play in?

a. Yellow shirts, blue shorts
b. White shirts, blue shorts
c. Yellow shirts, yellow shorts

57. Which country won Gold in the first ever Women's Olympic Soccer Tournament in 1996?

a. Germany
b. Japan
c. U.S.A.

58. How often is the Copa America (South American Championship) held?

a. Every two years
b. Every four years
c. Every five years

59. In what way did the Pontiac Silverdome, one of the U.S.A.'s 1994 World Cup stadiums, make World Cup history?

a. It was the first World Cup venue with a capacity of over 100,000
b. It was the first World Cup venue with an artificial field surface
c. It was the first stadium to stage a World Cup game indoors

60. Who captained the winning team in the 1994 World Cup tournament?

a. Romario
b. Dunga
c. Bebeto

SOCCER QUIZ ANSWERS

Page 32: 1.b, 2.b, 3.a, 4.c, 5.a, 6.c, 7.b, 8.a, 9.a, 10.c, 11.a, 12.b, 13.c, 14.b, 15.a
Page 64: 16.b, 17.c, 18.b, 19.c, 20.a, 21.a, 22.a, 23.b, 24.a, 25.b, 26.c, 27.a, 28.c, 29.c, 30.c, 31.a
Page 96: 32.c, 33.a, 34.a, 35.b, 36.c, 37.c, 38.a, 39.b, 40.a, 41.c, 42.c, 43.b, 44.b, 45.c, 46.a, 47.c
This page: 48.b, 49.b, 50.c, 51.a, 52.a, 53.b, 54.c, 55.b, 56.a, 57.c, 58.a, 59.c, 60.b

SOCCER QUIZ

INDEX

Answers to the offsides quiz on page 119:
1) Offsides (the offsides player receives the ball indirectly from the throw-in) 2) Not offsides (the offsides player is not interfering with play) 3) Offsides (he is in a position which gives him an advantage) 4) Not offsides (he dribbles through).

With special thanks to soccer players Brooke Astle, Carl Brogden, David Buckley, John Cox, James Peter Greatrex, Gemma Grimshaw, John Jackson, Sarah Leigh, Nathan Miles, Andrew Perkin, Leanne Prince, Peter Riley, Christopher Sharples, Jody Spence, Ben Tipton, Christopher White, Neil Wilson, and to their coach, Bryn Cooper.

Thanks also to John Scott, Susan Robinson and Alexander Robinson for their expertise and assistance with the American edition.

All library photographs were supplied by Allsport UK and Empics picture agencies.

First published in 1997 by Usborne Publishing Ltd, 83-85 Saffron Hill, London EC1N 8RT, England. Copyright © 1997 Usborne Publishing Ltd. The name Usborne and the device ⚑ are Trade Marks of Usborne Publishing Ltd. All rights reserved.

Printed in Belgium. AE.
First published in America in August 1997.